Bahadur Shah and the Festival of Flower-sellers

Mirza Farhatullah Beg (1883–1947) was born of Mughal stock in Delhi. Educated at the Dehli Madrassah, Hindu College and St. Stephen's College, Delhi, he was Director of Education in the State of Hyderabad. Later, he became the Registrar of the High Court of Hyderabad. A renowned research scholar and a distinguished humorist, Beg's essays are marked by rich imagination and informality of style. His language is one of the best specimens of Urdu as spoken in Delhi. Steeped as he was in the medieval modes of culture and the lifestyle of Delhi, he saw beauty in them and sought to make them live for good through his writings.

Mohammed Zakir was born in Delhi and educated at St. Stephen's College, Sri Ram College of Commerce and Zakir Husain Delhi College, University of Delhi. He retired as Professor of Urdu after four decades of service in the Jamia Millia Islamia, Delhi. His main interests have been translation, literary criticism and Urdu linguistics.

Bahadur Shah and the Festival of Flower-sellers

A translation into English of Farhatullah Beg's modern Urdu Classic

Bahadur Shah aur Phool Valon ki Sair

by

Mohammed Zakir

Orient BlackSwan

BAHADUR SHAH AND THE FESTIVAL OF FLOWER-SELLERS

ORIENT BLACKSWAN PRIVATE LIMITED

Registered Office
3-6-752 Himayatnagar, Hyderabad 500 029 (Telangana), INDIA
E-mail: centraloffice@orientblackswan.com

Other Offices
Bangalore, Bhopal, Bhubaneshwar, Chennai,
Ernakulam, Guwahati, Hyderabad, Jaipur, Kolkata,
Lucknow, Mumbai, New Delhi, Noida, Patna

First Published by Orient Blackswan Pvt. Ltd. 2012
Reprinted by Orient Blackswan Pvt. Ltd. 2014

ISBN 978 81 250 4618 9

Typeset in
Adobe Jenson Pro 11.5/14
by Eleven Arts, Delhi

Printed in India at
Yash Printographics
Noida

Published by
Orient Blackswan Private Limited
1/24 Asaf Ali Road
New Delhi 110 002
E-mail: delhi@orientblackswan.com

I would like to dedicate this book to my cousins and friends—Sheikh Mohd. Azam, Bha'i Momin Siddiqui, Noor ul Islam, Shakir ul Islam, Bha'i Tahir, Bha'i Sabir, Shahid ul Islam, Mohd. Ahmad, Mohd. Sultan, Salahuddin, Mohd. Mian, Mamun Usman, Bilal Ahmad, Mamun Jalil Ahmad Pari, Bha'i Zamir, Bha'i Anwar, Bha'i Muttalib/Aslam, Bha'i Zia ul Arifin, Ahmad Tariq Chaman, Zia ul Haq Chaman, Ahmad Mian Asghar Jamali, Ahmad Jamal, Naseem Ahmad, Bha'i Razi, Bha'i Mohd. Din, Ghausuddin, Mohd. Mursaleen, Bha'i Hamid Kamal, Mohd. Ahmad K. B., Aftab Ahmad, Bha'i Mohsin, Mamun Ghulam Ajiz and Mohd. Zahir. They are no longer alive but hardly are they gone from my heart.

I would also like to dedicate this book to Bha'i Zahir ul Islam, Ahsan Sheikh, S. M. Arif, Mohd. Farooq, Asrar ul Haq, Mohd. Aslam Noori, Mukarramuddin, Vilayat Husain Rizvi, Siraj ul Arifin, Ghulam Jilani, Abdul Naeem, S. Sagheer Ahmad, Noor Ahmad and Habibuddin.

How much we enjoyed growing up together before 1947!

Contents

Acknowledgements

Apart from its significant aspects, which of late have been taken note of, translation from one's mother tongue is an indication of one's love for it. This is how I have always felt. Besides the blended salty-sweetness of Urdu, the language, I think that others should share the aroma and richness of its literature as well. Translation is a lot like preparing a dictionary—it provides an opportunity to the coming together of two different languages and cultural communities. It is hard work but one that is immensely satisfying.

I am grateful to Mrs Naima Sultan, daughter of Mirza Farhatullah Beg, who on her own behalf and on behalf of other heirs of Mirza Sahib kindly gave me permission to publish this translation. I cordially thank Dr Gautam Chakravarty and Mr Ali Zaki, grandson of Mirza Sahib, for putting me in touch with Mrs Naima Sultan.

I have also to thank my friends, particularly Dr Anwar Ahmad Khan, Dr Aslam Pervez, Dr Mohd. Feroze, Dr Abdur Rasheed and the late Mr Mohd. Saleem who took interest in this work as it progressed. I also thank Mr Mohd. Asim and others of the Dr Zakir Husain Library, Jamia Millia Islamia, Delhi, for arranging for me the requisitioned books and other references.

My brother H. M. Fazil's help came in handy in understanding the fine architectural points mentioned in this work. Cousin S. M. Adil's comments were also timely and useful. *Shabash* to my daughter Rasheda Sultana and my son Tanzim ur Rahman for helping me in preparing the Glossary. Particular *shabash* to my son Mohd. Amin Salem who read out the manuscript as I sat typing and proofreading it. I would like to thank Ms Vidya Rao and Ms Rinita Banerjee for their editorial comments and seeing the work through press.

Mohammed Zakir

Introduction

Bahadur Shah and the Festival of Flower-sellers is a translation of *Bahadur Shah aur Phool Valon ki Sair* written by Mirza Farhatullah Beg (1883–1947) towards the end of the third decade of the last century and has been published several times. It has nearly become a little modern classic in Urdu. Apparently it is just a narrative-cum-descriptive essay about a woman making a vow and fulfilling it.

During the administration of the British East India Company, in early nineteenth century, it so happened that a prince insulted the British Resident in the royal court. Consequently, he was sent to prison. His mother, the queen, promised to present a *chadar* (a sheet of cloth) and a *masehri* (bed-curtain of flowers) as offerings at the tomb of a saint when her son was released. Upon his release these offerings were taken to the tomb of the saint in a procession in which both the Hindus and the Muslims participated with great zeal. The flower-sellers who made the bed-curtain of flowers also made a flower-*pankha* (fan), suspended with it. Akbar Shah II, the king, the Mughal emperor (practically a pensioner of the East India Company), not only made it an offering to be made regularly, every year, but also advised the Hindus to present a similar flower-fan as an offering at a historic temple near the saint's tomb. He wished that the Hindus and the Muslims participate in each other's offering ceremonies. It was, thus, actually 'flower offering' ceremonies but they came to be known as the festival of flower-sellers.

Making vows and offerings at the tombs of religious men and seeking help from them in mundane affairs pertains to a man's faith and religious beliefs. The ceremonies and the rituals that go with them, practised year after year, become the distinguishing marks of the culture of a people. Engaging in various kinds of outdoor activities such as wrestling and swimming competitions, swinging, display of fireworks, and setting up temporary stalls to sell toys, general merchandise and eatables, etc., during these ceremonies and rituals give them a touch of excitement and zeal that a fair has. The festival of the flower-sellers remained an annual feature with the Delhiites until 1942 when it was banned by the British government for security reasons. The realisation that such social events were indeed the cementing forces to bring about greater cohesion that could promote emotional integration among different communities, helped revive the festival in 1962 by Jawaharlal Nehru, the first Prime Minister of India. Now there is a registered Society, 'Anjuman Sair-e-Gulfaroshan', which organises it every year. There is every effort to make it more popular by introducing newer programmes in which more and more people can participate. Central and state authorities in Delhi also patronise it. It is also reported that some other states too are taking interest in this festival by sending their cultural troupes to Delhi every year. Indeed, such participation leads to overshadowing the regional diversities.

Empires rise, empires fall. Various events that happen during their reign, leave behind traces that become the hallmark of culture and civilisation. Between the thirteenth and mid-nineteenth centuries (i.e., between the time when the Muslim Sultanate was established and the time when the last Mughal emperor was deposed) India witnessed several such political, economic and social changes. I do not mean to dwell on these changes of course, but I would like to point out that perhaps the most important outcome of the intermingling of the two cultures—Indian (represented by various Indo-Aryan dialects in north India) and non-Indian (which was itself the result of the assimilation of Persian, Arabic and Turkish elements with Persian as its representative language)—was the coming to existence of a composite Indo-Muslim culture. Its most representative language came to be Urdu from the Indo-European family of languages, with some bearings of the Semitic and the Altaic. During the course of its development it was given various names at different times and at different places in India.

India has been like 'a seething cauldron', like 'a continent of some sorceress'. From time immemorial, whoever has come to settle here, has been naturalised as an Indian in due course of time. Hardly anybody can say with conviction that they could keep their original identities intact. We still find diversities that can be traced to the ancient and medieval settlers; however, it would not be wrong to say that there has been a sort of underlying unity or emotional integration that has been manifest in the religious thoughts and practices, and the customs and ceremonies followed by the people. In the later nineteenth century, the spread of education on modern lines gave a more pronounced sense of oneness among the people. During the later middle ages, Islam with its democratic tendencies—more manifest in Sufism which had by the thirteenth century become a movement with the aim of taking Islam to the masses—and more or less uninterrupted rule of Muslims (adequate/inadequate representatives of Islam) over vast territories with a uniform system of administration, must have also imperceptibly contributed towards this sense of oneness.

Muslims were conquerors, but they were settlers as well. To fulfil their political as well as everyday needs they had to rub against the local population, the previous settlers who had by then come to be naturalised as Indians speaking various dialects of the Indo-Aryan, the most important branch of the Indo-European. The spread of the conquerors/new settlers across the country gave a fillip to regional languages and along with it a new synthesised speech/ language which could serve both the new settlers and the earlier ones came to the fore. Thus, Urdu assumed greater significance, having a wider reach along with the regional languages with their defined and undefined areas, just as Sanskrit (after assimilating some Dravidian elements) must have assumed in ancient times and Prakrit in the early middle ages.

Urdu was rightly called 'the grand popular language of India', Hindustani being one of its several other names. Indeed, it had come to be the *lingua franca*. Over the centuries, there has been a large amount of literature in that language, both prose and poetry, which is essentially Indian in nature and secular in spirit truly representing the composite Indo-Muslim culture I speak of.

If India is not only to remain peaceful and prosperous but also be a leading light for all pluralistic societies, it has to keep this spirit alive and invigorate it.

Bahadur Shah,[1] the last Mughal emperor, was a true representative of the cultural synthesis, to whatever extent it may be, we have just hinted at. He also patronised the festival of flower-sellers and made it more exuberant.[2] I would also like to mention here, that contrary to perhaps several historians of Urdu literature, Bahadur Shah was a poet in his own right; students of Urdu literature who study his writings with an appreciating eye have to admit that he was. Apart from the simple language and a cultivated taste, his later *ghazal*s remind us of his personal sufferings and misfortunes. However these were not meant to be only lamentation and cry or about traditional mystical feelings. One also finds in them traces of his passionate love for freedom and a strong resolve to achieve it. Those who know about the racking circumstances he was placed in[3] and are also conversant with the symbolic nature of *ghazal* poetry will find significance in such couplets:

Bahar a'i asiran-e-qafas apas men kahte hain
pharak kar torna hai gar qafas tayyar ho ja'o

Spring has set in, the caged ones say to each other,
'Flap, flutter your wings
If you want to break this cage!'
* * *

Qafas ke tukre ura dun pharak kar aaj
Iradah mera asiran-e-ham-nafas yun hai

Oh my comrades here, in this cage,
It is my resolve
I shall flap and flutter my wings
Until this cage breaks into pieces!
* * *

Gar asiron ko yunhi sayyad tu pharka'ega
To nikal bhagenge voh ik din qafas ko tor ke

If you, the hunter,
Go on torturing the caged ones,
They'll break the cage
And fly away one day!
* * *

Besides poetry, Bahadur Shah practised other arts like archery and calligraphy as well which were popular in those days.[4] He was of a peaceful disposition and a disciple of a Chishti saint. It was at his instance that all the *vazifahs* (quiet repetition of an Attribute of Allah or a passage from the Holy Book) from the times of the Prophet of Islam till then were compiled in the form of a book to which a *taqriz* (an introduction by way of commendation) was written by the poet

Mirza Asadullah Khan Ghalib (which is a brief but a marvellous introduction to Sufism/mysticism itself).[5] It will be inadvertent for me to comment on Bahadur Shah's role in the 1857 Mutiny or First War of Independence. But I may well say that in spite of all the frivolities that generally go with despotic rulers and his personal weaknesses, Bahadur Shah had the qualities of heart which had made him popular with the masses. His, perhaps, is a unique example of how a monarch by force of circumstances beyond his control and by his own disposition comes to be a commoner among the commons sharing their pleasure and pain.

Some historical facts need to be also borne in mind. Before India passed under the British Crown (1858) there had been hardly any trace of communal feelings between the Hindus and the Muslims. The cohesion and oneness that once existed between the two communities gradually diminished. Later, there was even the parting of the ways. There were, in fact, many factors responsible for it, but with the downfall of the Mughal empire, the absence of the Mughal court which served as 'the standard of cultural behaviour' was certainly one, if not *the most,* important factor. It is also well-known that since the days of Emperor Akbar, certain Mughal emperors had Hindu wives. Bahadur Shah's mother was Lal Bai, a Rajput.[6] Before him, Shah Jahan and Shah Alam II had also had Hindu mothers.[7] Common sense tells us that there must have been a semblance, a streak of secularism or liberalism or openness or whatever it may be called, in the harem atmosphere at least because of their presence. 'The slow seepage of Hindu ideas and customs from the harem into the rest of the palace,' says Dalrymple, 'had led the later Mughal emperors to subscribe to particularly tolerant and syncretic form of Sufi Islam, aligned to the liberal Chishti brotherhood.'[8] Moreover, it should also be remembered that majority of the Muslims in India had been converts, and however zealous a convert one may be to practise his new religion, the age-old way of life to which he is accustomed does not change overnight. It not only persists but also overshadows the new doctrine and beliefs. Rightly does Professor Mujeeb point out that, '... while the conversion from Hinduism to Islam may have been a matter of moments, the conversion of the converts from the Hindu to the Islamic way of life took centuries, and it was during this process that Hindus and Muslims influenced each other. A study of Muslim customs, specially those relating to marriage and child-birth, would probably show that Hindu customs and ideas had a far greater hold on the Muslims than Islamic doctrine and practice.'[9]

Festivals of both, Hindus and Muslims, such as 'Eid, Dussehra, Diwali and Holi were celebrated in the Fort with equal fervour. I was told by the older members of my family that at least upto the mid-thirties of the last century Holi was celebrated in the clubs in the gardens adjoining Chandni Chowk in Delhi. Muharram and Basant were observed by both the communities together in certain cities of the native states. Bahadur Shah loved his subjects. He banned the sacrifice of cows during the days of the Mutiny so that it did not hurt Hindu sentiments.[10] Dalrymple aptly observes: 'while Zafar was certainly not cut out to be a heroic or revolutionary leader, he remains, like his ancestor the Emperor Akbar, an attractive symbol of Islamic civilisation at its most tolerant and pluralistic.... He is certainly a strikingly liberal and likeable figure.... He never forgot the central importance of preserving the bond between his Hindu and Muslim subjects, which he always recognised was the central stitching that held his capital city together....'[11] His subjects, both Hindus and Muslims, too, reciprocated his love. In the words of C. F. Andrews, 'his subjects knew well how ineffective he was, but they loved him all the same.'[12] This is why in spite of individual grudges against the East India Company or aspirations of different personalities who took to arms against it, it was the reluctant Bahadur Shah who was the common choice of the Hindus and the Muslims under whose name the struggle for freedom was carried out.

Indeed, the fall of Bahadur Shah was not the fall of Bahadur Shah alone. It also meant the fall of the old system, loss of prestige of the aristocratic order, and above all, the end of the leading centre of the composite Indo-Muslim culture which originated and developed in India and which I believe is her destiny.

***

The author of this essay, Mirza Farhatullah Beg, was born of Mughal stock in Delhi. Educated at the (Kashmiri Gate) Madrasa, Hindu College and St. Stephen's College, Delhi, he worked as a director of Education in the State of Hyderabad. Later, he became the Inspector General of Courts, Nizam's Government. Besides his interest in cricket,[13] painting and writing poetry, he also wrote plays. He published his essays under the title *Mazamin-e-Farhat* in seven volumes which include his pen-portraits, humorous writings and research articles on some medieval Urdu poets and writers as well. He also edited the poetical works of two medieval Urdu poets—Inamullah Khan, poetically surnamed Yaqin (d. 1755) and Vali Muhammad, renowned as Nazir Akbarabadi (d. 1830)—with critical Introductions.

Farhat was a well-known research scholar and a distinguished humorist with a style of his own. He started writing under the pen-name Mirza Alam Nashrah (Mirza, the Tattler) which speaks of his humorous disposition. Steeped as he was in the medieval modes of culture and the lifestyle of Delhi, he saw beauty in it and sought to keep it alive for good through his writings.

Urdu literature does not lack in such descriptive or narrative prose pieces as *Bahadur Shah aur Phool Valon ki Sair*. Several other writers have written about the *sair* itself. Faizuddin, who is said to have spent a greater part of his life in the service of a Mughal prince in the fort, has recorded various rituals and ceremonies in the fort during the reigns of the last two Mughal emperors in his *Bazm-e-Akhir* (The Last Assembly), first published in 1885. He also describes the *sair*, taking note of the royal procession and the din and bustle of the fair in a simple language. Another famous writer, Nasir Nazeer Firaq

(1865–1933) while speaking of the *sair*, concentrates on the description of the offerings made at the tomb and on the adornment of the royal ladies on that occasion.[14] But apart from the inimitable style of Mirza Farhatullah Beg and his excellence in bringing about a short but living glimpse of Bahadur Shah Zafar, the man, what distinguishes this essay from the rest is his genius in the presentation of a cultural event by nearly making it a social document as it vividly brings before us the rapport between a king and his subjects. His description of competitions between the people of the city of Delhi and the people of the Fort, whether it was swimming, or playing fireworks, or kite-flying is highly picturesque and charming. Farhat is equally superb in describing the formation and march of the royal procession, and the singing and swinging scenes of the royal ladies and princesses in gardens together with their cooking sweetmeats and the fun and frolic that accompanied it. Writings which preserve such social events may also be a good source in etching out the cultural history of a people.

Farhat's style is based on the use of ordinary matter of fact language as spoken in Delhi, with an unrestricted flow. But he is never trite in its use. It is always lively and refreshing. Translating a work of a writer having a distinguished style is always a challenge. Even otherwise, it is more or less generally agreed that one who has read the original in one's mother tongue, seldom enjoys it in translation. But then, who can deny that translation does help in the intellectual growth and development in the multilingual world? It is a bridge between two different linguistic and cultural communities which may lead to create a better sense of proximity and brotherhood among them. So one should go ahead with it undeterred, and so have I.[15] Many of the notes given after the text have been provided by me and have been marked as 'translator's note'. Where, along with the author's note (from the original), I have added some information I have separately referred to them as 'author's note' and 'translator's note'. The words given in brackets within the text and notes, are also mine.

NOTES

1. Mirza Abu Zafar Sirajuddin Muhammad Bahadur Shah II, poetically surnamed Zafar, the last Mughal emperor: born AD 1775; accn. AD 1837; deposed 1858 at the time of Sepoy Mutiny/First Indian War of Independence; d. 1862 at Rangoon [translator's note].

2. In the days of Bahadur Shah, the fair was held for three days in which more than a hundred thousand people participated and nearly Rs 3 lakhs was spent on it. Aslam Pervez, *Bahadur Shah Zafar* (Delhi: Anjuman Taraqqi Urdu, 2008), 289, with reference to *Dastan-e-Ghadr* by Zaheer Dehlavi, and *Bazm-e-Akhir* by Munshi Faizuddin.

3. For just a glimpse of it see William Dalrymple, *The Last Mughal* (Delhi: Penguin/Viking, 2006), 37–39.

4. For a brief account of Bahadur Shah's accomplishments (and pursuits) see Dalrymple, *The Last Mughal*, 2 and 100; also *Bahadur Shah Zafar*, 263, and Noorul Hasan Hashmi, *Dilli ka Dabistan-e-Sha'iri* (Lucknow: Idarah-e-Farogh-e-Urdu, 1971), 370.

5. Khwaja Altaf Husain Hali, *Yadgar-e-Ghalib* (Allahabad, 1955), 184–87.

6. *Bahadur Shah Zafar*, 59, and Dalrymple, *The Last Mughal*, 77.

7. Ijaz Husain (trans.), *Tarikh-e-Shahjahan* by Banarsi Pershad Saxena (Delhi: Taraqqi-e-Urdu Board, 1978), 41 (henceforth *Tarikh-e-Shahjahan*) and Imtiaz Ali Khan Arshi (ed.), *Nadirat-e-Shahi* by Abul Muzaffar Jalaluddin Muhammad Shah Alam II (Rampur: Hindustan Press, 1944), 5–6 (henceforth *Nadirat-e-Shahi*).

8. Dalrymple, *The Last Mughal*, 77.

9. M. Mujeeb, *Islamic Influence on Indian Society* (Delhi: Meenakshi Prakashan, 1972), xi.

10. Mutiny Papers Collection No. 142, File No. 144, National Archives of India as referred to in *Bahadur Shah Zafar*, 269.

11. Dalrymple, *The Last Mughal*, 483–84.

12. C. F. Andrews, *Zakaullah of Delhi*, Reprint (New Delhi: Oxford University Press), 2003, 8.

13. An interesting anecdote is related about his playing cricket at St. Stephen's College by Rev. J. G. F. Day who was on the staff of the college (1902–7). Describing him as an admirable fast bowler, especially when he took off his boots, he says, 'On one occasion an address had been given in

the College Hall on "Lift up Your Hearts". The next day a cricket match was being played and two of our opponents had become set. They were piling up a huge score, and our men were becoming discouraged. Suddenly Farhatullah, who was bowling, shouted "Lift up Your Hearts!" He then delivered a fast 'yorker', clean bowling our opponent's crack batsman. Ultimately we won the match.' (F. F. Monk, *A History of St. Stephen's College* [Calcutta: YMCA Publishing House], 1935, 103–4)

14. Nasir Nazeer Firaq, *Lal Qil'e ki Ek Jhalak* or *A Glimpse of the Red Fort* (Delhi: Urdu Akademi, 1986), 105–8.

15. Two other essays of Mirza Farhatullah Beg viz. *Dilli ki Akhri Shama'* (The Last Lamp of Delhi), also known as *Dilli ka Akhri Yadgar Musharah* (The Last Musha'irah of Delhi) and *Daktar Nazir Ahmad ki Kahani—Kuchh Meri Kuchh Unki Zabani* have also become little modern classics in Urdu. These have been translated by Akhtar Qambar and the present writer respectively and published by Orient BlackSwan under the titles: *The Last Musha'irah of Delhi* (1979), and *Nazir Ahmad: In His Own Words and Mine* (2009).

Bahadur Shah and the Festival of Flower-sellers

How aptly has Sa'di,[1] the poet said:

Ra'iyyat chu bekh ast o Sultan darakht
Darakht ai pisar bashad ar bekh sakht

People are the roots
And their Sultan, the tree;
A tree stands firm, my son,
If its roots are firm!

It was mainly due to the strong foundations that even the most powerful of rulers dared not think of dethroning the king of Delhi, although he had come to be a king only in name. The flourishing gardens of the city had been ruined by the ravages of time, the wafting winds of opposition had uprooted and devastated the mighty foundations of Mughal grandeur, many a misfortune had befallen the empire, and yet, no ruler could dare think of making Delhi a part of his territory. The Mahrattas had strived hard, the Pathans and the Jats too had tried their strength, and then the English had used their force—but the king of Delhi had remained the king of Delhi. And until Delhi was completely ruined, somebody or another in the royal family was always striving to usurp the throne. However much did the Resident[2] at Delhi wish to reduce the honour and prestige of the king, the Governor General[3] suggest to take possession of the Fort[4] by getting the royal family shifted to the Qutab,[5] and the Court of Directors (of the East India Company) propose to put an end to the existing kingdom—the members of the Board did not agree. They well knew the significance of the throne of Delhi and the extent of its influence. There were heated debates and discussions. The young and more ambitious officers were most keen. But nothing worked against the more experienced old men of England when Mr Mulker said in the meeting of the Board, 'Friends, for fifty years I have been in India. I know the conditions there. I know the importance of the Fort of Delhi. If its foundation extends to Kabul in the north-west, it goes to Ras Kumari in the south. If it extends to Assam in the east, it goes to Kathiawar in the west. If the Fort is touched, such an earthquake will come that the whole of India will be shaken. Let this kingship, which is only in name, continue as it is.' At last, the experienced won and the younger lot lost. No doubt, the prestige of the king of Delhi was greatly reduced, but the faith of the people in him remained unshaken. The king and the people shared their pleasure and pain with each other. The fact was that both knew, and knew it well, that they were one and the same; they belonged to each other.

Take the murder of King Alamgir II,[6] for instance. Just see how much did not only the Hindu men but also Hindu women love the king and how much regard did rulers from other kingdoms too have for him. Alamgir II had great faith in *faqirs* (ascetics or religious mendicants) and dervishes. Whenever he came to know of any *faqir's* arrival, he would invite him to the Fort. If the *faqir* did not come, the King would go to see him personally at his place and give him gifts. According to him, being kind to *faqirs* in this world was actually a means of making a provision for himself in the 'other' world.

Ghaziuddin was the vizier in those days in Delhi. Lord alone knows why he despised the king so much.[7] He could not dare think of laying his hands on him in the Fort and so he laid a trap to kill him away from the Fort. He gave out in the Fort that 'a pious man has come and is staying in the old Kotlah.[8] He is a man endowed with miraculous and divine powers; but neither has he gone to see anyone nor does he want others to come to him.' This excited the king and the people started to praise the Shah Sahib, that is, the pious man, all the more. Then, one night, the king went out all alone to the Kotlah searching for him in those ruins. Several men were already lying in ambush to kill him. Four of them came out of one of the domes, murdered the king and threw away his corpse on the sands of the river Jamna.

God Almighty be praised! A brahmin woman, Ram Kaur by name, happened to pass that way. Seeing the body she stopped for a while and immediately thought of running away from there. But then, when she carefully saw the body she realised that it was the dead body of the king! She sat there crying the whole night with the head of the dead king, that helpless martyr, in her arms. In the morning, the people who were on their way to bathe in the river Jamna, recognised that it was the king's dead body. The news of his death reached the city and left everybody shocked. The poor martyr's body was buried. Mirza Abdullah Ali Gauhar (b. AD 1728), known as Shah Alam II[9] now became king. He sent for Ram Kaur and gave her very many rewards and adopted her as his sister. A few days later, the *salono* festival[10] was celebrated. The 'sister' brought a *rakhi* made of pearls to tie on the wrist of 'her brother'. The king was pleased to let her tie the *rakhi*, and gave her and her relatives *khil'ats* (robes of honour). Thus *rakhi-bandhan*, that is, the festival of tying *rakhis*, became one of the ceremonies in the Fort. As long as the Fort flourished, there remained brotherly relations between the people of the Fort and the members of the family of the brahmin woman. Every year *rakhis* were brought and tied on the wrists of the king and the princes, and the members of the family of the brahmin woman were given robes of honour. This system was discontinued only when the king had to leave the Fort.

Phool valon ki sair or the festival of flower-sellers, was also the result of the mutual love between the king and his subjects. It so happened that Akbar Shah II[11] wanted to make his second son, seventeen-year-old Mirza Jahangir (b. 1790),[12] the heir-apparent. Sirajuddin, poetically surnamed Zafar, was the elder son but father and son were not on good terms with each other. Akbar Shah II was very fond of Mirza Jahangir. And why not? Mirza Jahangir's mother, Navvah Mumtaz Mahal, the Queen, was a powerful authority in the Fort. His Majesty and the Queen tried to get Mirza Jahangir nominated as the heir-apparent in the Residency. Mr Seton[13] was the Resident in those days. Never had such an Englishman come to India who respected the king so much. He had as much respect for Akbar Shah as he had for his own king. He would take off his hat at the place of obeisance to pay respects to the king. While in his audience he would never sit on a chair even if it was offered to him. He strictly observed the royal etiquette and always tried to fulfil the king's wishes. In fact, he would do everything for him but he would not approve of Mirza Jahangir to be the heir-apparent. Apparently, one reason was that he did not want to disturb the customary (Mughal) practice of accession to the throne. And secondly, he was not satisfied with the character and conduct of Mirza Jahangir.

Mirza Jahangir was a heavy drunkard and an extremely outspoken person. As he had a grudge against Mr Seton because of his opposition to him, one day he called him a bugaboo in the royal court itself. Mr Seton ignored it. But after a few days, Mirza Jahangir fired at him. How long could such activities be ignored? As a result, he was sent to prison in Allahabad. This came as a great shock to Mumtaz Mahal, his mother, the Queen. And so she made a vow to present a *chadar*, and a *masehri*, as an offering to be spread over the tomb of Khwajah Bakhtyar Kaki[14] when Mirza Jahangir was released.

God Almighty be praised! It was the noble Mr Seton who recommended that the Sahib-e-Alam,[15] Mirza Jahangir, was released from prison. And so, on his arrival in Delhi, the Queen made preparations to fulfil her vow. The *chadar* was taken with great splendour to the tomb. The Hindus and the Muslims of the whole city participated in it. A fair was held in the Qutab which continued for several days. The flower-sellers who made the bed-curtain of flowers also made a *pankha* (flower-fan) suspended with it. Sirajuddin Zafar, the heir-apparent composed a poem titled *Pankha*, 'The Fan', in its praise:

Nur-e-altaf o karam ki hai yeh sab us ke jhalak
keh voh zahir hai malik aur hai batin men malak
is tamashe ki na kyon dhum ho aflak talak
Aftabi se khajal jis ke hai khurshid-e-falak
yeh bana us shah-e-akbar ki badaulat pankha

Sha'iq is sair ke sab aj hain ba dida-e-dil
Vaqe'i sair hai yeh dekhne hi ke qabil
Chashm-e-anjum ho na is sair pe kyonkar ma'il
sair yeh dekhe hai voh begam-e-vala manzil
Jiske divan ka rakhe mah se nisbat pankha

Rang ka josh hai mahi se ze bas mah talak
Dube hain rang men madhosh se agah talak
Aj rangin hai ra 'iyyat se laga shah talak
Za'fran zar hai ik bam se dargah talak
Dekhne a'i hai is rang se khalqat pankha

All this is a glimpse of the soothing light of
kindness and benevolence of one

Who is apparently a king, but at heart
an angel;
Why shouldn't the clamour of this spectacle
reach out to the heavens?
Even the heavenly sun fights shy against
its dazzling *aftabi*[16] shield;
This fan has been made by the kindness of
King Akbar.

Everyone heartily desires to see this
spectacle;
It is worth seeing, indeed!
Why shouldn't even the stars be inclined
to see it?
They know that this is being watched
by the lady of high rank and dignity[17]
It is she, the fan of whose hall of audience
has a semblance with the crescent[18]

There's colour everywhere;
It is bubbling forth all over
from the *mahi*[19] to the moon;
Everyone, the sensible and the insensible,
is steeped in colour.
Everyone, from the subjects to the king,
is happy today;
From the rooftops of the houses
to the *dargah*[20]
It is all a field of saffron,[21] as though,
everyone has come to see the *pankha*
in a joyous, happy mood!

The king liked this fair very much. To the people of Delhi he said, 'What if we hold this fair every year in the beginning of the month of *Bhadon*?[22] The Muslims may present a flower-fan in the holy dargah (shrine of Khwajah Bakhtyar Kaki) and the Hindus in the Jog Maya Ji temple.[23] Let the Hindus participate in the offering of the Muslims and the Muslims participate in the offering of the Hindus. It will be a fair all right but along with it there will be the coming together of two communities.' Goodness needs no counsel. The citizens of Delhi readily agreed. And thus was laid the foundation of *phool valon ki sair*, the festival of flower-sellers. His Majesty, the King himself went to the Qutab and stayed there. The princes were also present.[24]

However, gradually the nature of this fair changed quite a bit. This song came to be very popular in those days:

Qutab ko chala mera Akbar hatila
Na raste mein jungle na milta hai tila

To Qutab goes my dear Akbar,[25] the stubborn fellow;
To him it matters little
Whether there's a jungle or a hillock on the way!

* * *

In the days of Bahadur Shah II, the fair came to be celebrated with such exuberance that it defies description. If you wish to really get a glimpse of how it was celebrated, please shut your eyes and I'll show you ...

The *Saavan* of AH 1264/AD 1848 was awful. First there was no rain and when it rained, it rained so heavily that there seemed to be water everywhere. Rain fell, unstoppable, for fifteen days—from Wednesday to Wednesday to Wednesday.[26] It rained cats and dogs. River Jamna had extended itself upto Nigambodh Ghat[27] and found its way into the city through the Kela Ghat. The Chandni Chowk canal[28] swelled out of its banks. What to say of small houses, even the big *havelis* and mansions made of brick and stone gave way. Sounds of falling houses could be heard everywhere—a bang here, a thud there. Here collapsed the roof of one, and there fell the side wall or the shed of another. Hardly was there any house whose *chhal*[29] at least had not fallen. The poor left their houses and came out in the open. Household goods were heaped up in front of Jama Masjid. While one placed his cot and covered it with a *dari* (cotton carpet) to make a roof, building a small hut, the other raised a curtain around a *chhapar-khat* (a bedstead with a tester and curtains) to accommodate the womenfolk. It was a strange sight of distress. Even two years earlier, it had rained very heavily causing the collapse of houses but this time it was altogether different. The *baniyas* (provision-sellers) had their share of difficulties and the *bhatiyaras* (the inn-keepers) had their's! Where could they go? What would they eat?

Bahadur Shah II was a king only in name. The entire administration was in the hands of the British, the East India Company. Why would the Company be concerned with the plight of the poor and distressed in Delhi? Let the people themselves manage their own affairs! Anyhow, His Majesty, the King, did what he could. All the Government houses were opened to shelter the people. The revenue of Kot Qasim[30] had been received during that time. He spent all of it on the distressed subjects. The Muslims were given food twice a day, while grain was distributed among the Hindus. Thus, somehow or the other, those days of distress came to pass. On the sixteenth day, the rains gave a respite; the sky became clear and a part of the sun could be seen. People were relieved. Two or three days were spent in repairing the houses and putting things in order. And then, the carefree thought of holding the fair.

How could it be that the Delhiites idly sit unexcited when the brimful Jamna flowed, boundless? It was proclaimed by the beat of the drum that there would be a swimming competition the next day. People began gathering before the Fort from early in the morning and by 9 o'clock the city was evacuated; the *belah*,[31] that is, the reclaimed riverine land, was full of men. The betel-leaf sellers, fruit-sellers, grocers and all the petty merchants put up their shops there. There were festivities everywhere, where just a day before stood a jungle. His Majesty, the King also took his seat in the Samman Burj.[32] Seating arrangements for the princes were made on the floor of the courtyard of the Diwan-e-Khas, the hall of Private Audience. *Masnad*s or cushioned seats were set for the ladies and the princesses against the lattices of Moti Mahal,[33] Khas Mahal[34] and Asad Burj. The masters of the art of swimming, together with their disciples, dived into the river Jamna and started to show their skills in swimming. While one swam flat just like a floating wooden plank, another swam upright in a way that even his knees could be seen above water, and yet another swam like a tiger against the flow of the water. While this went on, a kite-flying competition started between the people of the Fort and the people of the city. *Tukkal*s or small paper kites (of the rivals) coiled around each other and farther and farther they flew gyrated, entangled, far beyond the Humayun's Tomb.[35] Then there were other kites. A whole lot of them. The whole sky was covered with them. Seeing this, nobody could say that the city had been under so much distress just two days ago.

By the evening, the fair came to an end. By ten in the night the *belah* again turned into a jungle, just as it had been. Heaps of *dauna*s (leaves folded in the shape of cups for holding sweetmeats) and *abkhorah*s (earthen vessels to hold water), and the marks of *peek* or spittles of the juice from the chewed betel-leaf and skins of fruits, however, did remind one that there had been a big city at that place which flourished for a while and then disappeared.

* * *

The month of *Saavan* was over and *Bhadon* set in. The days of heavy rains were over. It was time for light, fine drizzles. The Delhiites again felt tickled. The greenery of the Qutab again came to their mind and they thought of holding the festival of flower-sellers. Two Hindus and two Muslims from amongst the elite of Delhi went to Lal Haveli[36] and sought the King's audience. They were ushered in.

They spoke of this and that, finally arriving at exactly what they had come to say, 'Your Majesty, the time for the flower-sellers' festival has come. The *jharna* (cascade) and the Shamsi Talab[37] are full to the brim with water, like the cups. Please fix a date. It will be our good fortune if Your Majesty also does us honour by your gracious presence!' The King said, 'Oh yes, my dears, it is right, your pleasure is my pleasure. Let it be the 15th of the lunar month. As for us, we shall certainly come. Why shouldn't we if you are there?'

As soon as the date was fixed, the *shehna'i* (a musical pipe) player of the royal *chauki* (band of musicians) presented himself with a silver trumpet. A pleasant note was played on it, and thus the fifteenth day was fixed to celebrate the flower-sellers' festival. The whole city came to know of it by the blowing of the trumpet. People started preparing for it. No sooner had His Majesty, the King, gone to the *Tasbih Khanah* from the special audience, that all the ladies and princesses started coming there. One by one they came and after paying their respects took their seats.

Within a short time all the ladies of the Fort gathered there but all of them kept silent. Their eyes, however clearly showed what they wanted to say: 'To the Qutab, please.' His Majesty knew what they wished for and said, 'My dears, I know what you wish to say. The date of the flower-sellers' festival has been fixed. It is the 10th (of the lunar month) today. The Festival will start on the 15th. It will be better if we are the first to go there. Otherwise, it will be inconvenient for the people of the city if we go after them. Go and enjoy there the beauty of the Qutab and then leave it for the Delhiites to enjoy. Now you may go and prepare for it. If God so wills, we shall start early tomorrow morning. And listen, my dear Dara,[38] you arrange for our conveyance. Inform the *kotwal* (chief officer of a city or town) and the *Qil'ah-dar* (commandant of the palace guard)[39] too. I'll tell Hakim Sahib myself.[40] If we start early in the morning, we shall reach the Qutab by the evening, if God so wills, after visiting Sultan Ji.'[41]

All the ladies who had assembled there to hear these words, left one by one after paying their respects. Preparations began.

They started packing goods and sending it to the *toshakchi* (the superintendent of store). It was not long that scores of boxes, hundreds of cloth-bound bundles and thousands of packets—in short, all kinds of trash, weighing many, oh so many, maunds was heaped up there. Some of it was loaded on bullock-carts, some on camels, and some of it was kept in *shikrams*[42] or camel-carts. It was about 12.30 in the afternoon that these carriages left one after another and by only about 2 this whole row came to an end. Hardly had the poor *darogah* (superintendent) heaved a sigh of relief when an *urdabegni* (armed female attendant in the harem)[43] conveyed the command of the King to him saying, 'Send the royal store just now; we shall stay in the Jangli Mahal in the Qutab. As such, there is no need to send the tents, *sara pardah*[44] and awnings. But if the people need and demand these things, these may be given to them. Don't wait for another command. Let this command be conveyed to the people of Delhi through Hakim Ahsanullah Khan Sahib.' As soon as this command was conveyed, the *darogah* again got ready and started to pack the royal luggage with his assistants.

Everywhere the men of administration were busy in some activity or another; it seemed as if they were making preparations for a marriage ceremony. While the *churiwalian* helped the girls put on bangles, others dyed the *dupattahs*[45] in light green colour, someone ground the *mehndi* (myrtle) and some other collected the frying pans and cauldrons. Neither food, nor sleep crossed their minds. This continued up to 12 at night. By 2 in the morning a bugle was blown, calling upon everyone to come out and ride on the carriages. The carriages were parked in the ground adjacent to the *naubat khanah*[46] in front of the Lahori Gate. All the female servants and attendants[47] took their seats in different kinds of carriages.[48] Even the spaces devised by setting bags of cotton net for keeping grass etc. at the back and front of certain carts were first stuffed with luggage and over those sat two or three dancing girls and maid servants. By hook or crook this problem was solved. Oxen were yoked to the carriages and thus the caravans started off for the Qutab. The torch-bearers with their torches and oil-containers in their hands, accompanied them. No sooner had these people left the Fort, that all kinds of vehicles and conveyances for the royal ladies were parked by the Moti Mahal.[49]

The heir-apparent also came out. The soldiers of the *daglah* (quilted coat) platoon closed the roads for the women's privacy. The Turkans (fair-coloured, armed Turkish women)[50] and the Gurjans (Georgean women) in uniform surrounded the place with screens of canvas. All the ladies as they came out were provided a carriage, according to their status. A *qalmaqani* (armed female attendant)[51] and an *urdabegni* were sent with every vehicle. It was around 3 when the first *rath* (four-wheeled carriage) started off. In the vanguard were the *rath*s and after them were other carriages. At the end was the *sukhpal* (palanquin) of Navvab Zeenat Mahal, the Queen. As the procession reached the Lahori Gate, Captain Douglas, the commandant of the Fort, came down and gave a salute.[52] When they went out of the Gate, one row of soldiers of the *daglah* platoon came in the vanguard and another row of soldiers at the rear. The armed female attendants, dressed like men, wearing turbans having an opening in front, and armed with all the seven weapons—bows, arrows, shields, swords, daggers, spears and guns—accompanied the carriages of the princesses on either side. Then there was the platoon of the Turkans who surrounded the carriages of the ladies. They were also dressed like men. Their curly hair were let loose on their shoulders and they had a small *'amamah* (a sheet of cloth) wound on their heads with a rising *kalghi* (plume) of white feathers on it. They had small spears in their hands, a *tarkash* (quiver) on their backs, *kamans* (bows) on their shoulders, swords hanging on their sides, and *pesh-qabz* (daggers) in their *dab*s (belts). It seemed as though an army of the Turks had entered Delhi.

The carriage of Navvab Zeenat Mahal[53] had a more stately look. There were two *habshans* (Abyssinian women) in the front who had curly hair. Their turbans were red with tassels of muqqaish (white silver thread) in them. Their lips were fat and eyes red, and they wore loose coats of red *gornet* (satin). With thin drum sticks in their hands they rode on horses. One of them beat the drum wrapped up in brocade put on the back of a horse ahead of her, and the other called out: 'Attention! Be vigilant! Long live Her Majesty, the Queen!' On either side of the *sukhpal* there were two Georgean women. One of them held a fan of peacock feathers and the other a *chanwar* (bushy tail of a Tibetan bull/cow) in her hand to fan and keep off the flies. On every step they called the name of God. At the end were the platoons of armed female attendants. They were dressed and armed like men. At short distances were women torch-bearers holding torches and oil containers in their hands. Some of the lamps were *doshakhah* (two-branched) and some *panj shakhah* (five-branched). Slowly they went along with the carriages. This procession proceeded up till the Delhi Gate in the same order. After passing through the Gate, the *raths* followed the road to the Qutab via the Turkman Gate, and other carriages stopped there.

It was four o'clock in the morning when His Majesty, the King awoke. He took *gur* (jaggery) sherbet and then eased himself.[54]

The *khansaman* (master of stores) served a sealed cup of *yaquti* (an electuary) to the King. He broke open the seal and after taking it he said, 'Well, have all of them left?' The *khansamam* replied, 'May Your Majesty be exalted! All the arrangements have been made. Mir Tuzuk (master of the ceremonies),[55] is at your command, Your Majesty!' Bahadur Shah said, 'Proceed then, in the name of God!' As soon as this command was delivered, a bugle was blown. A *tam jham* (a rough kind of sedan chair carried by two men) for the heir-apparent, a *takht-e-ravan* (a travelling throne erected on a platform carried on the shoulders of men) for Mirza Shah Rukh, a *bochah* (a chair-*palki* or a kind of sedan) for Mirza Fakhru[56] and a *havadar* (a moveable throne on wheels)[57] for His Majesty, the King, were parked by the *Diwan-e-Khas* (Hall of Private Audience). All the other princes and the progeny of the *salatin*[58] rode on horses. As soon as His Majesty, the King, rode on the *havadar*, the herald announced, 'Attention! Salutations! His Majesty, the King!' The princes unsheathed their swords and gave a salute. All others bowed down in respect to the king. The heir-apparent, Mirza Shah Rukh and Mirza Fakhru rode on their carriages following the king. One attendant behind the king opened the royal parasol and the other held a fan or *suraj-mukhi*, for shade. And so moved this procession towards the Delhi Gate of the Fort. There was already a row of soldiers outside the Gate. At the head of the procession was an elephant with the royal standard. It was followed by a camel with a kettledrum on it. Then, there were the Turk riders.[59] Behind the cavalry, there were raised wooden platforms of *raushan chauki*,[60] and then came Mir Tuzuk. Then there were the carriages of the progeny of the *salatin*. Princes rode on horses, Mirza Fakhru on his *bochah*, Mirza Shah Rukh on his *takht-e-ravan* and Mirza Dara Bakht on his *tam jham*. After them was the *dur-bash*.[61] After the *dur-bash*, was the *havadar* of His Majesty, the King. It was followed by soldiers arrayed in rows. At the end of the cavalcade were the servants of the Fort and a crowd of people, the common men, the subjects. On either side of the road there were rows of torch-bearers. In short, the line of carriages and conveyances which started from the Delhi Gate of the Fort[62] ended at the old Kotlah.[63] His Majesty's *havadar* had just gone out of the Fort when the *shuhdas*[64] (blackguards) cried, 'Please, Your Majesty! We also deserve something, your Majesty! May God bless and exalt Your Majesty ever more, Amen! May the sheltering shadow of Your Majesty guard us, *Dillivalas*, for a hundred and thirty years, Amen! May God bless the princes and the princesses, Amen! The festival of flower-sellers is coming, Your Majesty! May we also see its spectacle and rejoice by the kindness and grace of Your Majesty!' The King made a gesture to the attendant behind him. He distributed a handful of coins, throwing them from where he sat, and as the coins scattered on the street, the blackguards rushed to pick them up, some even jumping to collect them, lying full-body. While one stretched out his hands to reach the coins, the other spread out his shirt. It was difficult to move for some time till this confusion lasted. When the blackguards had collected the coins to their fill, they moved ahead blessing the king. The *havadar* also moved forward. People had already come to know that the august royal procession would pass on that route on their way to the Qutab in the wee hours of the night. From midnight itself there was a horde of people thronging the streets from Khas Bazar to Faiz Bazar upto the Delhi Gate of the city. Thousands of women and children on the rooftops and upper storeys of the houses had been waiting to get a glimpse of the royal procession. Everyone was anxious to see the king. As time was short, the bazars could not be decorated with mirrors, but the gates and the front of some houses and shops had been adorned and illuminated. The procession moved slowly. There was complete silence on the road but the eyes and faces of the people showed that they were all overcome with emotion. Even His Majesty, the King could not avoid but shudder while tears inadvertently flowed down his cheeks. Who could foresee that in even less than nine years, he would return to this very road? Who knew that he would one day be walking captive, surrounded by soldiers, witness to the unshrouded dead bodies of his sons and nephews lying all around him, the palaces ruined—nobody aware of the whereabouts of those that lived in them.

Passing slowly and quietly through those roads the procession reached the Delhi Gate. The guards gave a salute and the procession was now en route to Sultan Ji.[65] The carriages of the ladies which had halted there, also joined this procession. The bearers (of palanquins etc.) now went faster and reached the Purana Qil'ah before sunrise. The *havadar* of His Majesty, the King was parked before the Sher Shah mosque. There, his Majesty recited his obligatory prayers and *vazifah*.[66]

They stayed there for an hour or so and started again. The day had not yet fully dawned when they reached the Humayun's Tomb. Curtains were drawn for ladies where they got down in the tomb, for privacy. At the outer Gate the female bearers took the *havadar* of His Majesty on their shoulders and carried it to the inner Gate of the tomb. The floor of the front courtyard had already been carpeted and the couches had been set. His Majesty took his seat and after finishing his *vazifah* entered the tomb. Hundreds of royal family members lay there—sleeping the sleep of death. His Majesty prayed in front of every grave. He pointed out each and every grave to the princes who followed him telling them about who it belonged to. He also told them about their illustrious deeds and compared their conditions with his own and could not help breaking into tears.[67] After praying for the dead he again came to his *havadar* and his caravan proceeded forth in the order it had come. The *dargah* of Hazrat Nizamuddin Auliya was nearby. They reached there in a very short time. It is difficult to tell how deep the faith of the Delhiites is in Hazrat Nizamuddin Auliya and how they revere his shrine. Every person, no matter which community or sect he belongs to, bows down in respect; there would hardly be someone so unfortunate as to return from there without his wish fulfilled. Arrangements for the womenfolk had already been made. The *havadar* was kept at the *ba'oli*.[68] His Majesty got down from the *havadar* and performed ablution. The princes washed themselves too. Curtains were drawn against the niches of the *ba'oli*. As for the princesses, while one bathed herself, another just sat on the edge of the *ba'oli*, dipping her feet in the water. His Majesty came back to his *havadar*. A female attendant said, 'Your Majesty, the boys of the *khadims*[69] of the *dargah* are here. They seek permission to swim in the *ba'oli*.' His Majesty said, 'Oh yes, call them here. They do have a right. And they should have it.' No sooner had he said this, than a score or so of boys came in and bowed down in respect. They asked for permission and then climbed on the dome. From the steps of the *ba'oli* the ladies and princesses started throwing coins into it. As soon as a coin was thrown, one boy took a jump from the dome and dived into the *ba'oli*, and brought out the coin. This amusement continued for some time. Then, everyone went into the holy *dargah*. First, they prayed at the tomb of Hazrat Amir Khusrau[70] and then they went to the tomb of Hazrat Sultan Ji. His Majesty went inside the tomb. The ladies stayed outside and prayed at the door. One held the door-chain and prayed, the other rubbed the dust of the threshold of the tomb on her face; another recited the Holy Qur'an with her shirt spread. Someone started talking about the gold cup suspended from the dome of the mosque. 'Look, my dear,' she said, 'this cup is of pure gold. It is very heavy; must weigh many *sers*![71] In the days of our grandfather, an old woman in distress came to this holy *dargah* and humbly submitted at the tomb: "*Ya Hazrat* (Your Holiness). I have seven daughters, and I have not even a pice to procure food. How shall I stand the mountainous burden of marrying them? You alone can make it easy for me!" When she went to the *Tasbih-Khanah*[72] from there, the cup came down from the ceiling of the dome in her arms. She was overjoyed to take it and went back home. She married her daughters in a grand manner. And they lived happily thereafter. Now, there was a rich man in Delhi. When he learnt of this event, he also went to the *dargah* and prayed at the tomb. Then he went into the mosque. He stared at the cup for long but it remained suspended as it was. He got agitated. He called the labourers and asked them to raise a platform there. They started raising it but lo and behold! The higher the platform was raised, further up the cup would go. When the platform reached the ceiling of the dome, the cup disappeared. And when the platform was removed, the cup appeared as it was. True, greed brings evil luck. Not only did he not get hold of the cup, he also ended up incurring an unnecessary expenditure on raising and removing the platform.'

After praying at the tomb, His Majesty, the King, went to the tomb of Muhammad Shah[73] and to the graves of Mirza Jahangir,[74] Mirza Nili[75] and Jahan Ara Begum.[76] After praying for them, he came back to the *ba'oli*, rewarded the *khadims* of the *dargah* and distributed alms to the beggars. Then all of them took the road straight to Mansur's Tomb.[77] There they stayed for about two hours. They left the place at about 4 o'clock and reached the Qutab by the evening. The Jangli Mahal and Mirza Babur's[78] *kothi* (mansion) had been decorated already. Those who had gone straight to the Qutab, had set things in order. Meals had been prepared. They had now tired themselves out. After taking their meals and saying their prayers, they fell asleep and got up only at the beat of the drum at 4 o'clock the following morning.

The Jangli Mahal is really a *jangli* (unkempt) place these days. But there was a time when it was a large palace. It was quite large but Bahadur Shah II had extended it further by adding the Diwan-e-Khas (Hall of Private Audience), the Diwan-e-'Am (Hall of Public Audience), the *Khas* (special) Mahal, and the Bab-e-Zafar (Zafar Gate) to it. This Gate itself is a small palace. It is entirely made of red stone. The stripes, margins and the flowers in marble on its front wall have enhanced its beauty. It is around sixteen or seventeen yards high. There is a spiral staircase of seventy-seven steps on one side. Right on the arch is the royal *barahdari* (a place with twelve doors); it is here that His Majesty and the ladies took their seats and enjoyed the spectacle of the *pankhas*. Adjacent to this gate is the gate of the *dargah*. *Pankhas* were taken from the *jharna* (cascade) towards this place. On the first day the *pankha* to be offered at the Jog Maya Ji temple was taken in a procession. On the second day it was taken straight to the tomb through the adjacent gate. The *pankha* to be taken to the Jog Maya Ji temple was halted for a while before the royal gate and then taken to the Temple by the passage in front of the house of Hakim Ahsanullah Khan. The interior portion of Bab-e-Zafar was worth seeing. From the outer gate to the palace inside, it had seven *deorhis* (porches). On every porch there was a three-door room for the guards. The *daglah* platoon guarded the outer gate. On the porches inside, there were female guards—the *Turkans*, the *qalmaqanis*, the *urdabegnis*, the *shidans* (Abyssinian women) and the *Gurjans*.

With such strict vigilance who could dare enter the palace? Not even a bird could fly in there. After entering the outer gate a passage on the left near the first porch led towards the apartments of the men. In short, this palace was so large and had so much space in it that the whole of Red Fort could have been easily accommodated there and still there would have remained some empty space in it.

Now, all of this has fallen to ruin. Only Bab-e-Zafar has survived. By its magnificent gate, one can guess what a grand palace it would have been once. The following chronogram composed by the king himself is inscribed on the front side of the gate:

Ein dar-e-'ali chu shud muhkam
bina hasb-ul-murad
Guft dil sal-e-bina 'Bab-e-Zafar payindah baad'.
1264 AH

When the foundation of this splendid gate
was laid as one wished, the heart said,
'Its date of construction is:
Bab-e-Zafar payindah baad,
(May Bab-e-Zafar last long!)[79]

This gate would also have met the same fate as that of the palaces inside due to the ravages of time. It is only because the Department of Archaeology, Government of India, has taken it under its supervision that it still exists.

With the beating of kettledrum in the morning, there was a hustle in the palace. All the princes and princesses washed themselves, changed their clothes, said their prayers, took their breakfast and came to pay their respects to His Majesty, the King. They wanted to remind him that they had come to the Qutab to enjoy the sights and not to just sit idle. His Majesty had finished his *vazifah* by then. He returned their salutations and blessed them. He knew what they had on their minds and said, 'Well, my dears, where do you want to go? To the cascade or to the Qutab Minar?' All of them said, 'Let us first go to the cascade, Your Majesty. The sky is overcast, the cascade will be at its full flow; it will really be a good sight to see.' An armed watchwoman was at once ordered to make arrangements for privacy. The women soldiers of the *daglah* platoon closed the place. The female armed attendants guarded the paths, the

Abyssinian and the Georgean female attendants accompanied the ladies and the princesses. A crowd of nurses, *asils* (companions of noble stock), the *khavas* (the favourite attendants) and the *surriyats* (confidant slave girls) came out and went straightaway towards the cascade. The princesses first went to the *dargah* and prayed at the tombs. Then, passing through Mirza Babur's *kothi* they went into the woods. First they stayed at the Jahaz Mahal[80] on the banks of the Shamsi Talab. For miles together there was water and nothing but water except a small dome in its centre.[81] The sight of the water was so alluring that many of the princesses wished they could take a plunge into it. But then they thought that this might be an improper thing to do so without the permission of His Majesty, the King. They stayed there for a short while before going to the Auliya Masjid.[82] They said their *nafl* (voluntary prayers) on the *musallas* in the courtyard. Meanwhile, His Majesty, the King also came there along with the princes. His Majesty's *havadar* went ahead and the women followed. In no time they reached the cascade for it was so very near the Auliya Masjid.

If one had not seen the cascade in the days gone by, one had not seen anything worthwhile. Looking at it, one felt as if a piece of paradise had been put in Mehrauli.[83] Just see the ways of God! What was it made for and what it has become! Firuz Shah Tughlaq (AD 1351–88) had a dam built on the Shamsi Talab and brought its water to the Nau Lakhi channel which he got connected with the water lines of Tughlaqabad so that there would be no shortage of water in the Tughlaqabad Fort. But Tughlaqabad was ruined; the channel broke down and the water of the tank found its way into the jungle. This was the condition when in AD 1700 Navvab Ghaziuddin Firuz Jang Bahadur[84] built the dam at Shamsi Talab. He also built cisterns, canals and fountains. And thus he made it another paradise. However, gradually, the *barahdaris* (rooms with twelve doors), *dalans* (halls) and houses were built there; a boundary wall was constructed as well. Trees grew dense and high and came to be like big umbrellas over the cascade. Thus, in a very short time this place changed quite a bit. Water would trickle down from the dam in small currents—a reason why it came to be called *jharna*. The three-door hall adjacent to the dam was the soul of the cascade. The roof of this hall was hollow. Water from the dam first came into the roof which had built-in breaches. Through those breaches, the water fell in a way that it seemed that it was raining in the hall. In the wall in front of the hall, hundreds of niches had been made to put lamps therein. When the water fell like a sheet over the lighted lamps, it seemed as if someone had set the water on fire, as if there was a heavy shower of melting gold. There were thirteen conduits under the *munder* (coping) of the roof. Water came down on the eaves through the conduits. There was a big cistern under the eaves. Water coming through the conduits first spread on the eaves and then fell down with such force into the cistern that it seemed as if it rained heavily. There was an eight-yards long, two-yards wide and one-yard deep canal in front of the cistern. The water from the cistern rose up with great force to flow over into the canal. Where the canal ended, they had fixed stones, a smooth slope with beautiful carvings on them; the in-lay work seemed like fishes tossing on the sheet with water flowing over them.

Water from two other canals from the north and the south also joined under this sheet. As water flowed ahead, it was divided into three canals. The bigger canal ran through the *mandva* (bower) of the *barahdari*[85] and the two smaller canals ran outside the boundary after winding on either side of the bower. There was hardly a king from Muhammad Shah to Bahadur Shah II who did not construct a building in the area surrounding the cascade. Muhammad Shah built the *mandva* over the *barahdari* on the big canal. Shah Alamgir II built a five-door hall towards the south. Akbar Shah II built a double-hall towards the north. Bahadur Shah II built the *barahdari* in red stone on the remaining space in the centre and thus completed the cascade complex.

There were two things worth seeing near the cascade. One was the *phisalna patthar* (slippery stone) and the other was the *amarayyan* (mango-grove). The slippery stone reminded us of the innovative spirit of Muhammad Shah. This stone was about six-and-a-quarter yards in length and two-and-a-half yards in width. It was firmly fixed in a slightly reclining position adjacent to the eastern wall of the cascade. It was so smooth that as soon as one sat on it, one slipped down. During the flower-sellers' festival people had a lot of fun by repeatedly sitting and slipping over it. Poet Zauq[86] metaphorically refers to it in the following couplet:

Main kahaan sang-e-dare-yaar se tal ja'unga
Kya woh patthhar hai phisalna, keh phisal ja'unga?

How could I be expected to move away
from the threshold of my beloved's door?
It is not the 'slippery stone', that I will slip down.

Adjacent to the bower of the barahdari was the other gate of the cascade and then came the mango-grove. There are mango trees at other places also but here they looked delightful. They remained green by the water of the cascade throughout the year and had grown so dense that one could hardly see the sky through them. With the trees up above and grass below, the earth and the sky seemed to be made of green velvet. If the cascade presented a paradise to the eyes, the peacocks' screams, the papihas' calls and the cuckoo's cooing were paradise to the ears. In short, the cascade presented a strange sight that gifted a renewed enjoyment every season; and to each and everyone it gave a different kind of pleasure.

Now, the pleasantness no longer exists. The Shamsi Talab has been reduced to the size of a cistern. Now the dam is far away from it. No longer does the water trickle down. The canals have dried up. The cisterns are filled with the rubble of the ruined buildings. Trees bear no leaves and most of them have been cut down. The slippery stone has broken into pieces. Only a few buildings still stand. In a few days, however, even those will be gone. The cascade and the mango-grove will be things of the past. True, indeed: save God everything is fancy!

Anyway, as soon as His Majesty, the King reached the cascade, the female attendants placed the royal cradle with a cushioned seat in it. The *havadar* was taken near the cradle. His Majesty, the King, got down from the *havadar* and took his seat in the cradle. Two distinguished female attendants with fly-flaps made of peacock feathers in their hands stood behind him and two others started to gently push and pull the cradle. After resting a while, His Majesty said, 'Well, my dears, what do you propose to do now? To swim or to sing?[87] Well, some of you may stay here in the cascade area, and some may go to the mango-grove. Enjoy here, and there too. I am going to the mango-grove.' With these words His Majesty slowly walked down into the mango-grove through the door of the *barahdari*. Arrangements had already been made there. On one side, seats were set for the King and Queen. On the other side, cotton carpets, white sheets of cloth and woollen carpets had been spread on the floor and cushions were placed for the princesses. Scores of swings were put up on the trees. His Majesty, the King, sat on the throne. Following him, the others took their seats after paying their respects and looked forward to receive his permission to go to the swings.

The King said, 'Well, why keep the swings unoccupied? Put the pans on fire; go, swing, and eat as well!' Taj Mahal[88] respectfully said, 'Your Majesty, we have already made arrangements for it. Your good word is what is needed. Everything will be done.' With these words she looked towards the slave-girls who were awaiting command. Scores of frying pans were at once taken out and hearths were made under the trees. *Angithees* (fire vessels) were placed before some ladies. While one beat up the gram flour, the other mixed sugar in the flour to prepare *gulgulas* (fried sweetmeats in the shape of small balls), and another prepared to fry *suhals* (thick round fried sweetmeat) and *andarsas* (fried sweet balls with *til* or sesame seeds on them). While one looked after the things to be used in making the *golis* (small balls of *andarsa*), the other made *chhaj-khajur* (fried sweetmeat in the shape of a date). It looked as if a small bazar had come alive. When everything was thus ready, one of them went up to His Majesty, the King, and said, 'If Your Majesty be pleased, frying may be started.' His Majesty said, 'No, let them sit in the swings first, then start frying.' With these words he looked towards Navvab Zeenat Mahal and Navvab Taj Mahal. Both of them got up. Taj Mahal was not as beautiful as Zeenat Mahal. Zeenat Mahal—well, what shall I say? What a lovely face she had! None as beautiful as she! It was her matchless beauty of which the king had heard and married her. She was fair, like a rose petal, like *shihab*.[89] She had an oval face, big bright eyes and a long upright nose. Her brows were drawn of collyrium. She wore light green bangles, a rose-red *dupattah* with embroidered stars around her head that fell on the shoulders, red brassieres, and a short shirt and *paejama* of green brocade made of fifty-two *kalis* (triangular pieces) along with a well-knit pair of shoes. With richly collyrium tinged eyes, *missi*[90] on her teeth and lac-dye on her lips, it seemed that a fairy had come down from a fairyland in the mango-grove.

Zeenat Mahal saw Taj Mahal with a wry face. Taj Mahal gave Zeenat Mahal Begum angry looks. Both were helpless because it was the king's command. The swing before His Majesty, the King, had red and green silvery wooden *patris* (slabs) and silk ropes. Both the ladies took their seats on the slabs. Zeenat Mahal joined her feet and Taj Mahal began to swing. His Majesty, the King, said, 'Oh no, swinging quietly like this I do not like. Call Tirmunhi Khanam and Dildar.[91] When the begums are swinging, why should they remain in the cascade?' On these words two *urdabegnis* at once left and brought them from the cascade. The two had been bathing there. They were hesitating to present themselves in that condition before His Majesty, the King. But when His Majesty himself said, 'Come on, my dears, these are the pleasantries of the Qutab,' they took courage. Squeezing and drying their clothes they came forward and stood on either side of the swing. The princesses also came to give them company while they sang. As they started to sing *malhar* (the mode pertaining to the rainy season), the first *gulgula* (sweetmeat) was put into the frying pan. Tirmunhi Khanam and Dildar were courtesans, Taj Mahal belonged to the *dom* caste whose women used to sing before the ladies, but the voices of the princesses also did not lack in sentiment as compared with theirs. There was hardly anyone among them in the palace who did not know how to sing in the days of Muhammad Shah. Tan Ras Khan, the musician, had been employed to teach them. Taj Mahal too was admitted in the palace for this very reason. Tirmunhi Khanam and Dildar, the two sisters were in the king's audience because of their excellence in singing. Now they started singing while the ladies swung:

Jhula kin daro re amarayyan
Jhula kin daro re amarayyan
Rain andheri, tal kinare, mirla jhangare, badal kare
Bundiyan paren phuniyan phuniyan
Jhula kin daro re amarayyan

Do sakhi jhulen, do hi jhulaen
Char mil gaiyan bhul bhulayyan
Jhula kin daro re amarayyan

Who has put up the swing in the mango-grove?
Who has put up the swing in the mango-grove?

The night is dark;
On the banks of the pond
The peacock is screaming;
Black clouds are hanging low;
Tiny drops of rain are gently falling;
Who has put up the swing in the mango-grove?

A pair of damsels has taken to swing;
Another pair gently pushes and pulls;
All the four have thus joined together;
It's a riddle, a riddle!
Who has put up the swing in the mango-grove?

Ah, those melodious voices, steeped in sentiment, their exquisite singing, the song of the season, the pleasant weather—every leaf and branch seemed to echo 'who has put up the swing in the mango-grove?' The peacock flew down on the ground and danced in ecstasy. The birds on the trees chirped and twittered. The whole jungle echoed with the calls of the papiha and the cooing of the cuckoo. It seemed as if time had come to a standstill. Then suddenly, came the rain. Many ran for shelter. His Majesty, the King said, 'My dears, in the Qutab, why do you run away from the rain? It is just a shower of the month of *Bhadon*. Here it comes and here it goes! Come now, Dildar, begin some other song. And why are all of you surrounding this one swing? Go to the other swings as well. Eat, sing, be merry and enjoy!'

On these words all of them rushed towards the swings. Two or three of the swings were occupied by the children. The princesses occupied the other ones. When it was less crowded, by the swing of the queen, Dildar started to sing another song:

Suno sakhi sayyan jogiya ho ga'e
Suno sakhi sayyan jogiya ho ga'e
Main jogan tere saath
Suno sakhi sayyan jogiya ho ga'e

Jogiya baja'e bin bansri
Jogiya baja'e bin bansri
Jogan ga'e hai malhar
Suno sakhi sayyan jogiya ho ga'e

Jogiya ne chha'i jangal jhonpri
Jogiya ne chha'i jangal jhonpri
Jogan ne chhaya hai bides
Suno sakhi sayyan jogiya ho ga'e

Jogiya ne pahne lal lal kapre
Jogiya ne pahne lal lal kapre
Jogan ke lambe lambe kes
Suno sakhi sayyan jogiya ho ga'e

Listen, my dear friend, my lord has become a *jogi*!
Listen, my dear friend, my lord has become a *jogi*!
And I, a *jogan*, alas, am here with you!

The *jogi* blows the flute!
The *jogi* blows the flute!
The *jogan* sings malhar (the song of rainy season)
Listen, my dear friend, my lord has become a *jogi*!

The *jogi* now lives in a hut in the jungle
The *jogi* now lives in a hut in the jungle
The *jogan* is at another place away from him!
Listen, my dear friend, my lord has become a *jogi*!

The *jogi* now wears a red ochre dress
The *jogi* now wears a red ochre dress
The *jogan* has her long hair undressed!
Listen, my dear friend, my lord has become a *jogi*!

They enjoyed the hot fried sweetmeats as they swung. While one had an *andarsa* in her mouth, the other ate a piece of *suhal* and someone else choked with a *phulki* (a small cake of peas fried in oil) stuck in her throat. Yes, all this—but *malhar*, the song of the monsoon, went on uninterrupted. The rain had stopped and the clouds had dispersed. Droplets of water still fell from the leaves of trees with a dripping sound. As a drop of water found its way in a cauldron of hot, boiling oil, spurts of the hot oil flew on all sides. Someone cried out as a drop of hot oil fell on her hand. Another got it on her face. One exclaimed, 'Ooiey!' and the other stood up patting her bruised cheek. But the others caught her and made her sit again saying, 'Oh my dear, dear, no one should be so delicate; such a tiny droplet, after all, is a part of the game. No one quits and gives up frying like this.' The spectacle of children on swings was all the more delightful. Fried stuff was consumed the most by them. Two swings were occupied by the boys and the rest by the girls. With every swing the boys went up high, so high, oh God! The girls, however, sat facing each other on red and green thin wooden slabs and were gently swinging with their feet. *Malhar*, the mode of the rainy season, was rendered; the notes were discordant, but who cared. Quarrels around who got the swing for how much time also took place as someone would say, 'Enough, my dear, you have had the swing far too long. Now let me also have it!' In the meanwhile, the song went on uninterrupted; it was really interesting. Just see:

Amma, aru jaman ghule dhare
Amma, main nahin khati, meri man
Amma, tatta pani bhara dhara
Amma, main nahin nahati, meri man
Amma, dhani jora sila dhara
Amma, main nahi pahanti, meri man
Amma, bhai bhavaj milan khare
Amma, main nahin milti, meri man

Amma, sajan dola liye khara
Amma, main nahin jati, meri man

My dear mother,
Peaches and jaman mixed together are here;
My dear mother, I won't eat them.
My dear mother, warm water is here,
My dear mother, I won't take my bath.
My dear mother, the light green dress is ready here,
My dear mother, I won't put it on.
My dear mother, my brother and his wife
have come to see me,
My dear mother, I won't meet them ...

In short, from uncles and aunts to nurses and maid-servants, all were there to see her but the girl says that she does not want to meet anyone of them. Long at last, she says, 'My dear mother, my husband has come with a palanquin to take me with him,' and yet, 'My dear mother, I won't go!'

This is what was going on here. There at the cascade it was a delightful, yet different scene. As His Majesty left the cascade for the mango-grove, the princesses closed the doors and changing their loose trousers for the tight ones, dived in the cistern. *Dham*! One was diving, the other was just swimming flat, still another was standing in waist-deep water warring, by splashing water on others. Children presented a noisy scene as they stood in the shallow canals. Some girls were taking their bath in the three-door hall of the cistern. Some of them were playing on the 'slippery stone' and tumbling they would come down on the ground. As they smothered themselves in mud, they took a plunge into the cistern. Those bathing there cried and asked them to get out of the cistern and not make the water dirty. Everyone was so absorbed in what he or she was doing that they were hardly aware of anything else. Meanwhile, it was learnt that His Majesty was going to Nazir Bagh. At once all of them came out of the water, hurriedly changed their dress and dragged the children out of the canals. But children were children, after all. As the ladies delayed a bit in taking out their clothes, they again plunged into the canals. With great difficulty they dried the children and changed their clothes. The doors of the cascade were opened and they went into the mango-grove. For a while they enjoyed the swings, ate some fried stuff, and then went to Nazir Bagh.

Nazir Bagh was just near the cascade. It was built by Roz Afzun, the Khwajah-sara (the eunuch in charge of the seraglio) of Muhammad Shah. Its main gate opens towards the mango-grove and the following chronogram giving the date of its construction is inscribed on it:

> *Pa'e tarikh-e-saalash guft hatif*
> *Khuda yare buvad bi-'illah mubarak*
>
> About the date of laying out of this garden,
> An angel said, 'May God bless it!'[92]

The garden had a pucca boundary wall. Inside the garden there were four *barahdaris* in red stone on all the four sides and a grand beautiful *barahdari* at its centre which had four cisterns on each side. These cisterns had several fountains in them. Water from the cascade flowed into the garden. Four canals had been dug out from the four cisterns. Each of them ran a little distance and then fell into another cistern. Then again, from there it ran a little distance before falling into another. Thus did these canals flow out after running through all the cisterns and round the *barahdaris* in front. The garden was thus divided into four parts because of these canals. On either side of the canals there were pucca paths. Adjoining them were plots of grassy patches. Adjacent to these plots were flowerbeds and tall, dense and shady trees. It was the beginning of *Bhadon*. The mango trees were in full bloom. They were all laden with ripe mangoes like the *gondni* (sebetan plum) trees. But who could dare touch them without prior permission? Fearing in heart, they asked for permission from His Majesty, the King. As soon as it was granted, all of them rushed towards the trees. The mangoes were half-eaten, half wasted and thrown away; their stones and skins too were playfully thrown at each other.

Thus, in no time all of them spoiled their clothes. They again bathed in the cisterns of the *barahdari*, changed and then sat down to eat. But how could they take anything now? They had already stuffed themselves with fried sweetmeats and mangoes. They just took a bite or two, and within a short time the table-cloth was folded up. And then, again, all of them went hurriedly towards the mango trees—eating, wasting and playfully throwing the mango stones and skins on each other. Several times everyone changed their clothes before evening set in. The entire day was spent between the cascade, mango-grove and the garden till they tired themselves out and retired to the Jangli Mahal. There they lay down to have a quick nap to get up only in the morning.

* * *

The following day they enjoyed the sights of the Qutab Minar, Ala'i Darvazah,[93] the tomb of Imam Zamin,[94] Bhim ki Chhitanki,[95] Karva Meetha Neem,[96] and the graves of the Twelve Kings.[97] On the third day they visited Chahal Tan Chahal Man,[98] Baka'oli's Fort,[99] the tombs of Jamali[100] and Kamali and Andheria Bagh.[101] They visited every nook and corner of the whole Qutab Complex in three days. By the end of it all, they were badly tired and settled down only when their feet blistered. The 14th of the lunar month had also come. Only Jangli Mahal and Mirza Babur's *kothi* remained under the occupation of the people of the Fort while other places were occupied by the people of the city.

The people of Delhi had prepared for the flower-sellers' festival throughout the year but after the announcement of the date they quickened the pace. The day the date was fixed, the *karkhandars*, that is, owners of petty cottage industries, pooled together whatever they could contribute according to their financial positions. The amount thus collected was meant for the expenses to be incurred on food and provisions in the Qutab. About other expenses it was 'each according to his liking'. The evacuation of Delhi started from the 13th of the lunar month. Shops were built from Ajmeri Gate to the Qutab. The palanquins of the rich and the *rath*s of the courtesans were seen on their way to the Qutab. Each *rath* was so beautiful as to invite the evil eye. It had a small velvet dome with flowery patterns embroidered in gold thread over it and a golden ball at the top with tassels made of satin and the strings made of twisted gold and silver threads, and extra white wheels with flowery patterns on them. The oxen were of Nagpur breed; they had embroidered cattle-cloth on their backs, strings of tiny silver bells round their necks, metal ornaments wrapped up on their horns and silk nose-strings. Inside the carriages sat the courtesans, well-adorned.

One after another, the *rath*s went. The elite of Delhi rode on horses—their saddle-cloth made of silver and gold threads and laces sewn in them. There were silvery and gold ornaments round their horses' necks, their manes well-dyed and neatly combed. Their grooms were wearing bright clothes and small red caps, and held silk reins in one hand and *chauhri*s (fly-flaps) in the other. The riders showed their feats of horsemanship as they rode along. On the other hand, the poor people presented a different sight. They had tied only a *tehmat* (a long loose cloth to be tied round the waist)[102] on their waists. Neither had they put on shirts, nor caps, nor shoes. A small earthen pitcher, however, was there put upside down on their heads, and they galloped fast. What shall I say what all was there in the pitcher? Suffice it to say that it had all that was needed while going to enjoy the flower-sellers' festival at the Qutab. It had their best clothes, an embroidered cap beautifully laced, a pair of richly embroidered *salim shahi* shoes, some money and a bedspread. Everything was there in it. It was all kept in the pitcher lest things got wet in the rain. It was a good idea. Everything remained safe and the pitcher was to be used in the Qutab.

They started for the Qutab on the morning of the 13th (of the lunar month) and this continued till the 14th evening. The whole of Delhi was evacuated. Hardly a house remained where a man or child was left. As for women, they enjoyed in the city itself. They went to the *sabzi mandi* (a locality formerly marked by its fruit gardens), enjoyed the sights there, rode on swings, made fried sweetmeats, ate mangoes to their fill, and bathed in cisterns. They fulfilled all their wishes. It was a royal command to open the gardens for the women of Delhi, arrange for their privacy, appoint guards outside the gardens so that no man could enter there and the womenfolk could freely enjoy themselves. The women too did full justice to the gardens and left all the trees stripped of mangoes! They ate the mangoes, piling up their stones and skins in heaps. More than once these were swept away but they were there to be swept again.

At the Qutab, the people, fond of amusement as ever, first found out places to settle. At a place like the Qutab Complex space was no problem. There were Government camps, royal houses and old ruins. The rich stayed in their own houses. Those who could afford took the upper floors on rent on either side of the main Mehrauli road. Some of the poor people stayed in the tents, camps and Government houses. Some stayed in the cascade Complex and some settled in the Nazir Bagh. But those who really wanted to enjoy the Qutab, stayed in the open. If it rained, it did not matter. Such was verily the fun at the Qutab.

It is difficult to find words to describe the scene at the Mehrauli bazar. From one end to the other it was decorated with mirrors. All sorts of petty merchants had established their shops. The whole bazar was filled with fruits, sweetmeats and toys. The *halva'is* (confectioners) were preparing salties and sweetmeats. The whole bazar was filled with the rich smell of eatables being baked or fried.[103] And the customers were jostling against each other. They purchased the eatables, ate them and threw away the leaves on which these eatables were served. Then they went to the shop of the *panvaran* (the female betel-leaf seller). With her well-combed oily hair, collyrium-tinged eyes, and *missi* powder on her teeth, she was sitting with a great poise and preparing betel-leaves to be chewed. The *desi* kind of betel-leaves wrapped up in a red piece of cloth were placed before her. People were purchasing the betel-leaves and as they were prepared by the *panvaran*, they cut jokes with each other. The jolly good ones purchased the betel-leaves for themselves and their friends chewed them, spit the juice, and left. Further on, they purchased wreaths and garlands of flowers from the flower-sellers and wore them round their necks. Then they stayed by the *saqi*,[104] had a pull or two at the *huqqah*, paid him a pice or two and walked away. The *saqi* too appeared to be somewhat different. His *huqqah* looked quite amusing. Its *nechah* (tube) was about a yard high and the *chilam* (fire-pot) was as big as to hold more than a quarter *ser* of tobacco. Its *nae* (pipe tube) was covered with *khas* (scented grass), and strings of fragrant *motiya* and *chameli* flowers were wound round it. It was so long that several *ghoris* (wooden supports) were arranged to hold it. On the supports were fixed tiny glass lamps in them. The *saqi* himself was clad in white and wearing a Banarasi *selah* (turban with one end hanging loosely from the shoulders on the body), with a red *patka* (sash) round his waist. He offered *huqqah* to everyone and straightened the pipe-tube to make it reach out even to those who were on the first floor of the buildings. Everyone enjoyed it. As one of them put his lips on the mouth-piece of the pipe-tube, the *saqi* recited the following couplet:

Huqqah jo hai huzur-e-mu'alla
ke haath men
Goya keh kahkashan hai surayya
ke haath men

The *huqqah* which your exalted self holds
Is like the Milky Way
In the hands of the Pleiades!

As evening set in, the bazar became overcrowded with people. If one threw a saucer, it wouldn't have fallen on the ground but would pass over their heads! Just after the sunset there was a trumpet call from the cascade. It meant that the *pankha* procession had begun. Everyone, therefore, went towards the cascade. People who were not able to find enough space there, were coming back. There was great rush. The stronger ones among them faced these pushes on their chests or backs, and the weak moved to one side making way for others saying 'let it go, why take the trouble. We shall see it when it comes this way.'

The procession started from the cascade and came on the road to Mehrauli. Torches, lanterns, glasses, chandeliers and *diwar-giri* (wall-lamps) had already been lit. There was so much light that it seemed as if it was a bright day. The procession moved forward in the bazar. The drum-beaters, clad in silver-laced green loose shirts, wearing red caps, one having a *dhol* (full drum), and the other a *tashah* (semi-spherical drum) hanging from their necks, beat the drums so hard with short wooden sticks that the sound deafened one and all. Behind them were two flags and pennants of brocade with tassels of gold and silver threads. The strings were made of twisted gold and silver. At the upper end of the flags there were octagonal-shaped lanterns of multi-coloured glass. On the top of one lantern was a golden crescent and on that of the other was a silvery circle. And then there was the Sharful Haq's horse, the *kotwal* followed by a row of policemen. Next was a *takht* (wooden platform) of *naubat-khanah*, large enough to be called a *barahdari* with musical instruments on it. A *barahdari* of bamboos on wooden planks was raised; a semi-dome like structure with wooden splinters on it, wrapped up with cloth and *panni* (thin metal leaf) was made. Finally, they had adorned it with paper flowers, and drew the curtains of marigold on its doors tightening them with strings. Those who played the instruments sat inside the *barahdari*. This platform, big enough to be called a house, was lifted by the bearers on their shoulders and taken along in the procession.

The *naubat-khanah* was followed by the people of the wrestling grounds of the city of Delhi. Every group had a *ustad* (master) and almost twenty disciples with well-built bodies, broad chests, strong, muscular and fleshy arms above the elbow, and lean waists. They wore short tight wrestlers' drawers and small amulets of gold round their necks. All of them tried to display what they were good at—while one whirled a stick around his head, the other exercised with the lezim, still another showed off how good he was with the sword. Where on one side they showed a competition in *phari-gatka* (the use of shields and fencing sticks), on the other they displayed their skill in club-fighting. In short, these 'wrestling grounds' were spread over a long way. They were followed by the trumpeteers along with the water-carriers of the city of Delhi. The latter wore extra white clothes with a short piece of red coarse cloth tied around their waists, and green silk turbans on their heads. They were ringing their well-cleaned sparkling shallow brass cups to the tune of the trumpets and drums. The trumpeteers were followed by persons who had red and green staffs in their hands. Fifteen or twenty of them were in a circle. In the centre thereof were *sarangi* players and drummers. The rapping sound of their striking staffs with each other following the rhythm of the beat of the drums was just marvellous. Then followed the 'moving thrones'. On these thrones were the dancing courtesans wearing costly *pishwaz* (long tunics made of fine cloth) coming down to their knees, embroidered *dupattah*s on their heads and *ghungroos* (anklets with several layers of the metallic bells strung together) on their ankles. They were followed by the English band and the troop of Turkish riders wearing uniforms of red *banat* (a broad piece of cloth) with white cuffs and collars. They had on their shoulders steel nets and had put on black breeches, long *luk* (patent leather) boots and red turbans. The riders held spears in their hands. The horses were moving slowly forward together. Following the riders there was the royal *raushan chauki* and the group of those who enjoyed the spectacle. All of them were clad in clean clothes and embroidered caps, *angarkhas* (long tunics of long bodice), one-breadth loose *paejamas* (trousers), and *salim shahi* shoes. After them, in four rows were the *bachhera*[105] platoon of fair, young boys—wearing light green turbans with small rising plumes. The coats were green[106] with breeches of white satin. They wore English black leather boots. Holding small spears with green flags on them, they marched with grace. They were followed by a large number of celebrities and nobles of Delhi who wore long gowns and cloaks. The Hindus among them wore small caps, yellow in colour, and the Muslims had caps pointed on four-sides and had saffron coloured cloth wound on their heads. They held *jaribs* (staffs) of different colours in their hands. They went along, all sprightly, garlands around their necks, strings of *molsiri* flowers of delicate fragrance tied on their wrists; they enjoyed the atmosphere, gracing the fair with their presence. They were followed by a group of royal *shehna'i*-players who played the notes of the season effortlessly. Enwrapped, they went along with the others.

And at the end was the floral *pankha* followed by a crowd of the flower-sellers and others.

Oh! That procession and the floral *pankha*. It was quite large, no doubt, but it was, after all, a thing made of mere splinters of bamboo with a thin metal leaf wrapped over it. Only tiny pieces of mirror were studded on it. It was decorated with paper flowers and hung over just a bamboo stick. But just think: it was not just a floral *pankha*; it was verily a symbol of intense love and emotional integration which had brought the Muslims, high and low, poor and rich, and the members of every community and of every class at one place. It had brought even the King out of the Fort to a village, Mehrauli. It was not merely a fan but a repository of faith and mutual love. Mehrauli was not just a village, but a big *lagan* (trough) in which the king himself was the candle and his subjects devoted moths.

The entire procession moved slowly on the Mehrauli Road under the soft drizzle, flapping and fanning themselves with scented *khas* fans. The bandsmen and the trumpeteers stayed before every door, played a tune or two, got rewarded and moved forward. The procession then reached the royal gate. The King came into the balcony of the *barahdari* above. *Chilmans* (screens) of split bamboos were drawn for the privacy of the ladies. Now all of them concentrated and came before the Bab-e-Zafar. There was a big plain ground in front of the gate where the bandsmen showed their skills, the men from the wrestling grounds displayed their feats, water-carriers rang their shallow brass cups, the men holding small staffs showed the mastery of their art, the courtesans performed exuberant dances. Everyone got a reward that suited their status; where one received a silk cloth for a turban, the other got a pair of shawls, yet another got a turban cloth with silk and gold threads, and another got *karas* (massive gold rings to be worn on the wrists). Meanwhile, the floral *pankha* also reached there. The elite of the city paid their respect to the King. Rose and fragrant *keora* water was sprinkled from the *gulab-pash* on all of them by those who were seeing the spectacle from the floors above. Scents and betel-leaves were offered to the elite. As the King gestured, the heir-apparent came down, garlanded them and saw them off. At this stage the sons of the *salatin*, and the princes too, joined the procession. It was about noon when the floral *pankha* reached the Jog Maya Ji temple.

The Jog Maya Ji temple is about two-hundred and fifty steps away from the Qutab Minar. It has a long boundary and small domes on its corners. It has twenty or twenty-two buildings in it. In the centre there is the *isthan* (shrine) of the Devi. It is said that the goddess was Sri Krishna's sister.[107] Legend has it that she had turned into lightning and disappeared, and settled here. Raja Yudhishtira, the eldest son of Pandu, built the temple but it had fallen and levelled to the ground. When the festival of the flower-sellers began, Lala Sedo Mal built a new temple with the consent of the Mughal emperor Akbar Shah II. By and by other buildings also came up within the enclosure. Now, it is a well-inhabited place. The peculiar thing about this temple is that a bedstead or a cot cannot be taken into it.

It was about one in the morning when people returned after making the offering of *pankha*. The next day the *pankha* of the *dargah*, the shrine of Hazrat Qutbuddin Bakhtyar Kaki was also taken out with equal splendour. It also stopped before Bab-e-Zafar. Some intimate friends tried to convince His Majesty, the King so that he may also join the *pankha* procession and accompany it to the *dargah*. But this was in vain; His Majesty did not agree and said, 'Well, my dears, please try to understand. When I did not go along with the *pankha* procession to the Jog Maya Ji temple, how can I join this procession to the *dargah*? How shall your Hindu brethren feel? They will think that as I am a Muslim, I joined the *pankha* procession of the Muslims; they will feel that I take them to be "others" and not my own for I did not even go down and kept sitting in the balcony. No, no; I shall behave alike to both of them. The princes went and joined the procession, so even now they will go and participate in this procession. As for the display of fireworks, both the Hindus and the Muslims participate in it, and they will.'[108]

The *dargah*[109] was close. After performing the *pankha* offering ceremony, people were free by ten at night. Straightaway they went to the Shamsi Talab. A short while later, His Majesty, the King's carriage also arrived. Screens were drawn on the Jahaz Mahal for the ladies. They took their seats behind the screens. The King came on the mehtabi (open high terrace). The favourites of the King and most of the nobles of Delhi were also called up.

All the spectators settled on the banks of the *talab* (tank). Hundreds of *bujras* (pleasure boats) and *nivaras* (barges) had been already arranged in the tank. The royal firework-makers embarked on half of them and rowed to one side. The remaining boats were occupied by the firework-makers of Delhi and the enthusiasts. They were rowed to the other side. As soon as His Majesty, the King arrived, both parties got ready for the competition.

After a short while, a *mehtabi* (a firework whose light when played, resembles the moonlight) was played on the Jahaz. This was, so to say, the beginning of the battle. First, balloons were released in the air. And in no time, it seemed as if thousands of suns and moons had appeared in the sky. When they were free from it, they took to playing the fireworks of war.[110] With the roaring sounds of the *hava'is*,[111] *chehkas*,[112] *lattoos* or tops,[113] *khatangas*[114] and *qalams*[115]—it seemed as if a big battle was being fought there.

Here, while the sky witnessed the fight of the fireworks, on water another competition had begun. Fireworks were being played on the pleasure-boats. Those boats were, so to say, like small warships; and the *mehtabis* and *chhachhuddars* were the guns; *chakkars* and the *khatangas* were the bombs, and the *anars*, *mastols* or masts of those 'warships'; soldiers made of dust with their bellies filled with gunpowder and *chhachhundar* in their navels with a chain of *sitabahs* from one end to the other in them were the fighters. From one side the boats of the people of Delhi, and from the other the boats of the people of the Fort were rowed towards each other. In the middle of the *talab*, it was all sound and fury as if it was really a war on the seas. The whole Tank and its banks were illuminated by the light from the fireworks. Their reflection on water, the shadows of the boats, the bare bodies of the players of fireworks, the crowd that had gathered on the banks and the noise, their faces yellow in the light of the fireworks and up above them a cloud of smoke—everything taken together had created a strange, frightening sight.

As soon as this ended, other fireworks were employed—*mehtabis*, *aftabis*,[116] and *anars*, *sehras*,[117] *jahi-juhis*,[118] *hat-phools*[119] and *charkhis*[120] were in a fight now. Then, boats of the two sides closed in and were rowed in front of the Jahaz Mahal. Here, the master firework players showed their perfection and skill. The nasri they played was so artfully made that it raised itself a hundred times while rolling on the ground and intermittently 'breathed'. The *batashah anar*[121] went hundreds of yards high and sparkled like flowers; and the unique thing about them was that even if they were played in the palm of a hand, they would not leave behind any scar at all. The big *anars* were just wonderful, the bright sparkling light oozing out of them as they went up, rising higher than the Jahaz Mahal. It seemed as if cypress trees planted in the boats were on fire. As they went up, it seemed as if there rained flowers; so lasting and powerful was the impact that it seemed that they would never die out. These did not even stain the clothes. Due to the bright light of the fireworks, it seemed as if the water had turned into gold; looking at the reflection of the fireworks on water, it seemed as if someone had laid out a fiery garden on the banks of the Shamsi Talab!

It was past midnight when this spectacle ended. Shawls, *mundils* (turbans of silk and gold threads) and pieces of silk turban cloth were distributed amongst the people on behalf of the King. Hence, everything got over only by three. Thereafter, everyone headed wherever they had put up due to the festival. His Majesty, the King, left the Qutab in the night itself and after visiting Raushan Chiragh Delhi[122] reached Delhi by the afternoon. Early the next morning people got up and purchased fruits and sweetmeats, *parathas* (loaves baked in *ghee* and of several layers) and *chhallas* (rings)[123] and toys. In the pleasant cold of the morning all of them left the Qutab for their homes. By the evening Mehrauli was deserted and Delhi regained its lively self.

So, did you see the festival ...

* * *

This was the festival of flower-sellers. Delightful it was! But alas! What can I say about the events that followed and the present condition? Owing to the Mutiny, Delhi was ruined and Bahadur Shah was deported to Rangoon. It was like a tie that had broken loose. What was once bound, now lay scattered. The tie that was, was of love; now there is a tie—but it is that of law.[124] Now every petty affair is taken to the law courts. The flower-sellers' festival was the manifestation of faith of the subjects in the King and of the love of the King for his subjects. The festival was celebrated even after the King but it gradually lost its former vitality because there was no centre now, and there was lack of emotional integration. For the last five or six years it has altogether stopped. If conditions, as they are now, continue and the discord persists as it is now, know then that it has stopped for good:

Ab ham-nashin main roun kya agli suhbaton ko
Ban ban ke khel aise lakhon bigar ga'e hain

But why should I cry, my friend,
    for those harmonious relations of the past,
Thousands of such wonderful ties were there
    But then they came to an end ...

* * *

The End

Well, the story is over. When read, it may lead one to wonder whether the events narrated here are real facts or were just fictitious, concocted stories. In this connection, I think it will be proper if I explain certain things. So far as the historical events and the sites and places as mentioned here are concerned, nobody should have any doubts about them. One may, however, think about the other events. In this regard, I would like to say that so far as the events related to the cascade and the mango-grove are concerned, I have heard about them from the old women who were themselves present in those social gatherings. Those who had seen and participated in the festivities in those days are still living in Delhi. They will certainly confirm each and every word I have written. I have seen the picture of the procession in the house of my teacher from whom I learnt painting. The only thing I have done is that I have blended them together and given them a particular colour. As for the conversations and dialogues in the text, well, that is of course the result of my imagination. But considering the relations and the bond of love between the subjects and the king in those days, even these dialogues cannot be taken as exaggerated. If you even get to read C. F. Andrews' *Zakaullah of Delhi*, you will yourself know. Mr Andrews was my teacher (at St. Stephen's College). I know how much trouble he had taken to interview the old men in Delhi and collect information from them about the events before the Mutiny. I also know how much he was himself impressed by it.

Now only one thing remains to be explained. And that is, why have I chosen the period AH 1264/AD 1848? Well, there is a valid reason for it. Up till that year, Bahadur Shah II (aged 73 years) had led, more or less, a peaceful and relaxed life. Only a year later, a miserable life awaited him. Dara Bakht, the heir-apparent died (in 1849). Mirza Shah Rukh had already passed away in 1847. Mirza Fakhru passed away (in 1856). The King himself had been poisoned. Then there were disputes about the nomination of Jawan Bakht as heir-apparent. By the time the 1857 Mutiny began, these worries and misfortunes had broken the aged king. It is because of these considerations that I have chosen AH 1264/AD 1848 as the last year when the king was free from such worries and misfortunes.

It is the trust of the old generation which I have laid before you. Now it is up to you to accept it or otherwise.

*Appendix**

Earlier, during the days of the East India Company, when Mr Seton was the Agent in Delhi, a girl of tender age was kidnapped from a slave-seller[1] and sold to Mir Madari, a eunuch, who kept trained singers and dancers. He brought her up and had her taught music. He named her Sarvari. Her father somehow traced her and petitioned against the eunuch in the court of Mr Seton. The eunuch in his statement said that he bought the girl from the girl's father who was a *faqir*. The girl also refused to recognise her father. The staff of the court was in collusion with Mir Madari who was rich, and his other *nauchis* kept the men of status entrapped in their coquetry. So all the witnesses told the court what the eunuch asked them to say.

However, in his heart of heart, Mr Seton was not convinced by their statements because he wondered why a poor person like the

* This story is an adaptation from *Nata'ij ul Ma'ani*, 35–37.

petitioner would file a false suit against such an influential person like Mir Madari. So, he called him to his residence and asked him the name he had given to his daughter. It was Khatoon, the *faqir* said. On the next hearing in court, Mr Seton asked the peon to call Khatoon to present herself. As soon as this name was called, the girl appeared. When cross-examined, she said that she was indeed called by that name when she was a child. The other witnesses fumbled and tried to give meaningless replies. Thus the truth came out. The guilty were punished and the girl was entrusted to her father.

NOTE

1. 'In the disorder and decadence characteristic of the middle nineteenth century Indian states, it was nothing uncommon for a girl to be kidnapped and sold.... such girls were bought by people who wanted domestic servants or courtesans who kept brothels or trained singers and dancers'; *Islamic Influence on Indian Society*, 'Umrao Jan Ada', 161.

Notes

BAHADUR SHAH AND THE FESTIVAL OF FLOWER-SELLERS

1. Sa'di was the poetical surname of Muslihuddin (AD 1175–1291), the great Persian poet; author of *Gulistan* and *Bostan* [translator's note].

2. The Resident was appointed by the British East India Company. The whole territory of Delhi was treated as a province or *subah*, of which the Resident was the *subedar* (Percival Spear, *Twilight of the Mughals* [Delhi: Oriental Books Reprint Corporation, 1969], 88) [translator's note].

3. The Governor General was appointed by the British East India Company [translator's note].

4. I am referring to the Red Fort in Delhi. It was built (1639–47) by the Mughal emperor Shah Jahan (accn. 1627; deposed 1658; d. 1666). He had named it *Urdu-e-Mu'alla*, the Exalted Camp. In the days of later Mughal Emperors, Akbar Shah II and Bahadur Shah II, it also came to be known as *Qil'ah-e-Mu'alla*. People also called it *Lal Haveli* [translator's note].

5. The Qutab Complex at Mehrauli, is 11 miles away towards the south of the city of Delhi. It is famous for its greenery and the ruins of the Delhi Sultanate (AD 1200–1400). People went there for a change of climate, sightseeing and to pay homage to the Chishti saint Khwajah Qutbuddin Bakhtyar Kaki (d. AD 1235) or visit the Jogmaya Ji Temple [translator's note].

6. Azizuddin Alamgir II (accn. 1754; killed 1759) was also a writer. He compiled *Majmu'ah-e-Rozgar* and *Muntakhabat-e-Azizi* (*Nadirat-e-Shahi*, 43) [translator's note].

7. The titles bestowed upon Ghaziuddin (b. 1737) were Imad ul Mulk, Ghaziuddin Khan Bahadur, Firuz Jang, Mir Bakhshi, Amir ul Umara, Nizam ul Mulk Asif Jah. He was the grandson of Mir Qamaruddin, Chin Qilich Khan, better known as Nizam ul Mulk of the Deccan and Asif Jah I (d. 1748) who had 'established a virtually independent kingdom ...' (R. C. Majumdar, H. C. Ray Chaudhuri, and Kalikinkar Datta, *An Advanced History of India* [London: Macmillan, 1950], 529). Ghaziuddin Imad ul Mulk's father was also known by his titles Ghaziuddin Firuz Jang (J. N. Sarkar, *The Fall of the Mughal Empire*, Vol. I. (Calcutta, 1932), 446–47 as quoted in Spear, *Twilight of the Mughals*, 13 and 237). Thus, there were three Ghaziuddins. Ghaziuddin I was the father of Nizam ul Mulk Asif Jah I (d. 1748, the founder of the independent kingdom of Hyderabad), who died in 1710 and was buried in the surroundings of the tomb he had himself built in Delhi and where Madrasah Ghaziuddin was established in 1692; this much later came to be the Delhi College. Ghaziuddin II (d. 1752) (*Fikr-e-Nau*, Zakir Husain, College Magazine, Special Number 2005–6) was the son of Nizam ul Mulk. Ghaziuddin III was the grandson of Nizam ul Mulk. Spear observes that Imad ul Mulk 'thenceforth sank into obscurity' (ibid., 14). He died in 1800 (Hashmi, *Dilli ka Dabistan-e-Sha'iri*, 10). Imad ul Mulk, was an 'ambitious' and 'unscrupulous' man. He had himself placed Alamgir II on the throne after blinding and deposing Ahmad Shah in 1754. He got Alamgir II killed (1759) because he attempted to free himself from his control. It was again he who 'compelled Shah Alam II, the successor to Alamgir II, to move as a wanderer from place to place ... and had to throw himself ultimately on the protection of the English and live as their pensioner till his death in 1806' (Majumdar, Ray Chaudhuri and Datta, *An Advanced History of India*, 529–30; also 537–38) [translator's note].

8. Ruins of the Palace of Firuz Shah (1358–88), about half a kilometre away towards south of the Delhi Gate of the city [translator's note].

9. See *Nadirat-e-Shahi*, 6; Accn. 1759; blinded 1788; d. 1806 (Spear, *Twilight of the Mughals*, 13–14; see also Majumdar, Ray Chaudhuri, and Datta, *An Advanced History of India*, 529, 537). Mirza Abdullah Ali Gauhar was a poet and writer. His poetical surname was *Aftab* (and also *Shah-e-Alam*). He composed in Urdu, Persian and Hindi (also Punjabi). He also knew Arabic and Turkish. (*Nadirat-e-Shahi*, 9). His collection of poetry *Nadirat-e-Shahi* is in both the Urdu and the Nagri scripts, and he has given *rag* and *tal* or the musical modes with certain poems. His poetry throws some light on the relations between the subjects and the king. His *'Aja'ib ul qisas*, a tale in prose, i.e., *dastan*, was recently discovered and published [translator's note].

10. A Hindu festival on the day of full moon in the month of Saavan (July–August). It is marked by the *rakhi-bandhan* ceremony, that is, tying of a thread on a brother's or another's wrist as a preservative against misfortune or as a symbol of mutual dependence. Legend has it that much earlier than this, Rani Karnavati of Mewar had sent a *rakhi* as a gift to Humayun (d. 1556), the Mughal Emperor, and solicited his assistance against Bahadur Shah of Gujarat [translator's note].

11. Mughal Emperor (b. 1760; accn. 1806; d. 1837); poetical surname *Shu'a* (which means rays of the sun) [translator's note].

12. See *Nadirat-e-Shahi*.

13. Seton, Archibald (Charles Theophilus Metcalfe, *Two Native Narratives of the Mutiny in Delhi*). An interesting case decided by him has been recorded which shows the man Seton was. Please see Appendix [translator's note].

14. A great Sufi saint (d. AD 1236). Also see note 11 [translator's note].

15. 'Sahib-e-Alam' was one of the several honorofics bestowed on princes [translator's note].

16. An embossed shield shaped like the sun [translator's note].

17. The poet refers to the queen here [translator's note].

18. It is a large wooden frame (here, crescent in shape) covered with a piece of cloth, a part thereof hanging down, suspended from the ceiling and pulled by string; it is used as a fan [translator's note].

19. People in India and Persia believe that, *mahi* is the fish on which stands the cow on whose horns the earth is supposed to rest. Mirza

Jahangir was sent to Allahabad twice as a political prisoner. During the first imprisonment he put up a very good behaviour and was soon released. He came to Delhi and was given a command of 1300 soldiers. It must have been at this occasion that his mother, the queen, fulfilled her vow and these celebrations were held. But he misbehaved again and was sent to Allahabad where he eventually died in 1821 (Spear, *Twilight of the Mughals*, 73–75) [translator's note].

20. A shrine or a tomb of a saint [translator's note].

21. It is said that the sight of a saffron-field excites laughter [translator's note].

22. The fifth month of the Saka era corresponding to August–September [translator's note].

23. Pl. see p. 38 of the present text.

24. According to one who had served as an *amil* (revenue official) in district Mukandpur (Riwan) during the reign of Akbar Shah II, 'all the princes, nobles and the English officials were asked to participate in the procession.... In the beginning there used to be only one *pankha* but later, all the artisans made their own *pankha*s separately showing their distinct craftsmanship and offered them at the shrine....' He also recalls an incident that shows the extent to which the spectators enjoyed the *pankha* procession and how the benevolent got overzealous in rewarding the artisans in the procession. He says, 'Once Kunwar Ajit Singh, the younger brother of the ruler of Patiala, Maharajah Karan Singh (accn. 1813), was seeing the procession. When they came with the *pankha* just before his apartment, he gave them a thousand rupees as reward. The second fan was that of the firework makers. They were also rewarded a thousand rupees by him. There were seven *pankha*s in that procession. He gave out seven thousand rupees in all. And he distributed among others whatever money was left with him. The administrative officer apprehended lest the money showering should lead to the loss of someone's life. Getting down from his elephant, he came to the Kunwar and said to him, "Please do not shower money like this. In running to collect it, someone may be killed in the scramble and thus you may earn disrepute instead of a good name." Only then did the Kunwar stop....' Naushahi, Gauhar (ed.), *Nata'ij ul Ma'ani by* Mehmood Beg Rahat (Lahore: Majlis-e-Taraqqi-e-Adab, 1967), 99–100 [translator's note].

25. This refers to King Akbar Shah II [translator's note].

26. It is believed that rains which begin on Wednesdays stop only on a Wednesday [translator's note].

27. A *ghat* is a place for bathing or a place for washing clothes on the bank of a river [translator's note].

28. Chandni Chowk was the 'central thoroughfare' of Delhi. A canal ran through the middle of it [translator's note].

29. A piece of wall [translator's note].

30. Kot Qasim is now a village 99 kms away, towards the south-east of Delhi in Rajasthan [translator's note].

31. The jungle near the sands of the Jamna where the *Jha'u* grew was known as *belah. Jha'u* is a type of tree which grows on marshy or sandy land [author's note].

32. It is an octagonal dome adjacent to the *Tasbih Khanah* in the Red Fort. Its proper name is *musamman* (octagon) but the Delhites call it Samman Burj [author's note]. *Tasbih Khanah* is an apartment or building for private worship [translator's note].

33. Private apartments in a palace [translator's note].

34. Apartments in the Red Fort [translator's note].

35. The tomb of the Mughal emperor Humayun (d. 1556), 3 miles away from the city of Delhi.

36. Lal Qil'ah or the Red Fort of Delhi, is also called Lal Haveli or only *Haveli*. The poet Hafiz Abdur Rahman Khan poetically surnamed *Ihsan*, says:

Miri tankhwah luti in luteron ne haveli men
duha'i hai Bahadur Shah Ghazi ki o duha'i hai

These swindlers have looted my salary in the Haveli
I appeal to Bahadur Shah Ghazi
Help, please help!

37. Shamsi Talab/Tank was built by Shamsuddin Iletmish (AD 1211–36) in AH 627/AD 1229–30. Ala'uddin Khilji (AD 1296–1316) got it cleaned in AH 711/AD 1311 and Firuz Shah Tughlaq (AD 1351–88) got it repaired in AH 752/AD 1351. Sharif Husain Qasmi (ed. and trans.), *Sair ul Manazil* by Mirza Sangin Beg (Delhi: Ghalib Institute, 1982), 261, fn

with reference to *Futuhat-e-Firuz Shahi*, 12 and Barni's *Tarikh-e-Firuz Shahi*, Vol. I, 241. Henceforth *Sair ul Manazil* [translator's note].

38. Mirza Dara Bakht, the heir-apparent; he died in 1849 at the age of 57. Spear, *Twilight of the Mughals*, 58 [translator's note].

39. Captain Douglas was the commandant of the palace guard. He was killed in the Mutiny. Spear, *Twilight of the Mughals*, 201 [translator's note].

40. *Ihteramuddaulah, 'Umdatul Hukama', Mu'tamid ul Mulk, Haziq-uz Zaman* Hakim Ahsanullah Khan *Sabit Jang Bahadur* was the grand vizier. It was on his witness that the poor king had to go in exile to Rangoon.

41. The Delhiites call the locality of Nizamuddin, Sultan Ji [author's note]. It is so called because of the tomb of the great Chishti saint, Nizamuddin Auliya (d. AD 1325). Also see note 65 [translator's note].

42. Formerly, a camel-cart was known as *shikram*. Later, this term was used for a horse-carriage as well.

43. The *urdabegnis* also managed the palaces and conveyed commands. They were not only clad like men but their names were also like those of men. They talked like men (using masculine gender for themselves, perhaps). Although they were women, from their appearance and manner they looked like men. In Delhi they were called *hurdabegnis* (gadabouts). Later, the word came to be used for such girls who were very naughty and quarrelsome and to whom the following couplet of Sauda (Mirza Rafi Sauda), an eminent Urdu poet (d. 1780) may apply:

Ladki voh ladkiyon mein jo khele
na keh laundon mein ja ke dand pele

The girl is one who plays with girls
And not one who takes exercise of dand*
with the boys.

(* *dand pelna*—an athletic or gymnastic exercise where one places the hands on the ground and then bends down as almost to touch the earth with the breast.)

44. A wall of canvas screens surrounding a cluster of tents (as used here) [translator's note].

45. A sheet of cloth to cover the head, shoulders and the bosom [translator's note].

46. The chamber where the time of the day or night was indicated by the beat of drums [translator's note].

47. The author mentions the following: *annas* (nurses), *mughlanis* (needle-women), *khavases* (favourites of the royal ladies and princesses), *chhokris* (dancing girls), *laundis* (slave girls), and *surriyats* (girls who kept secrets).

48. The following carriages are mentioned: *bharkases* (carts), *manjholis* (medium-size carriages) and *bahelis* (small, two-wheeled vehicles without springs).

49. The following types of conveyances are mentioned: *dolis* (a litter; a type of sedan), *neemahs* (semi-palki; only one person can sit in it), *miyanahs* (a *palki* with curtains, larger than *neemah*), *palkis* (palanquins), *chau-pahals* (these are *palkis* in shape but squarish, not rectangular), *chaudols* (a sort of sedan with two poles), and *sukhpals* (a kind of palanquin).

50. In the later days of the Mughals, immigration of the families from Turkestan, Ethiopia and Georgia had stopped. Female guards were now recruited from the families who had settled earlier in India. All of them were clad and skilled like men. Their duty was to guard the palaces.

51. The *qalmaqanis* worked as guards and also conveyed commands. They were not allowed to marry.

52. Please see note 39.

53. Navvab Zeenat Mahal was not of royal stock. In his old age the king had married the daughter of Navvab Shamsheruddaulah (of the family of Navvab Ali Quli Khan). It was God's grace that they had a son from their marriage who was named Jawan Bakht. Efforts to get him nominated as heir-apparent raised disputes which led to cleavages in the Fort. The king was so fond of his Begum that he did whatever she asked him to do. These cleavages, at last, took the king to Rangoon. Whenever, the Queen went outside the Fort, a drummer accompanied her. That is why she was called 'the lady with a drum'. She lived in the Fort for very short periods. She had got built a new palace at Lal Kuan

for herself. After the Mutiny, this palace was given away to (the ruler of) the State of Patiala. Now, that too is gone [author's note]. (At present, it accomodates a Government school for girls [translator's note]).

54. Everyday, after waking up, Bahadur Shah would take *gur* sherbet and vomit it out at once. It was believed that in this way the body would be cleansed of all the waste materials—helping it stay healthy.

55. Mir Tuzuk was a high rank official in the Fort. His was the job of looking after the arrangements in the royal court like processions and ushering in people for audience with the king. He was the only person who was allowed to have a *jarib* (staff) in his hand in the court. He would strike the staff on the foot of anyone who faltered in observing the etiquette of the court. This job was retained for a long time in the family of the Urdu poet Sa'adat Yar Khan whose pen name was Rangin (1756–1834).

56. Mirza Fakhruddin was proclaimed heir-apparent in 1849 after the death of prince Dara Bakht. But he died in 1856 [translator's note].

57. The seat is placed on an elephant to ride on [translator's note].

58. Distant relations of the ruling king. They were the descendants of former emperors going right back to Shah Jahan [author's note]. Shihabudin Shah Jahan; accn. 1627; deposed 1658; died 1666. In 1848 they were more than 2000 in number. Spear, *Twilight of the Mughals*, 62 [translator's note].

59. The section of the Delhi army clad in the English uniforms and armed with English weapons was called the Turk riders because the Turks had also the same attire in those days.

60. Literally, 'a lighted station'—a band of musicians with small pipes and drums [translator's note].

61. Literally, 'Stay away! keep distance' [translator's note]. It was a large, beautifully coloured log, studded with small spears. It was kept ahead of the king's carriage to guard against any possible attack on him.

62. The Lahori Gate and the Delhi Gate are the gates of the Fort. Two of the gates of the Delhi city are also named the same [author's note]. Other gates of the city were: Ajmeri Gate, Calcutta Gate, Kabuli Gate, Kashmiri Gate, Mori Gate, Rajghat Gate and Turkman Gate [translator's note]. The Lahori Gate, which stood at the end of Bazar Khari Ba'oli, has been levelled to the ground. Today, the Delhi Gate still stands at the end of Faiz Bazar. A road to the Purana Qil'ah, Old Fort, runs through it [author's note]. Purana Qil'ah is said to be situated at

the same site where Inderpat/Indraprasth of Pandavas flourished. The Mughal emperor Humayun (d. AD 1556) got it repaired and named it Din Panah. Sher Shah Suri (d. AD 1545) also built a mosque and other buildings in it. Much later, the mosque was repaired by Lord Curzon and the tank in its courtyard by Amir Habibullah of Afghanistan (*Asar-e-Delhi*, 48) [translator's note].

63. Please see note 8.

64. Literally, a blackguard of a city. But it is said that in those days it was almost a fashion and *shuhdas* were entrusted to lift the bedstead of the king. It was their habit to invoke blessings for the kings. See *Delhi College Magazine* 1959; article '*Dilli Valon ke tafrihi va ghair tafrihi Mashaghil*' by Syed Manzoor Ali Hashmi, Syed Muhammad Akhtar and Abdul Wadood Azhar. Also see *Farhang-e-Asi fiyyah*, Vol. 11, Taraqqi-e-Urdu Bureau, 1987) [translator's note].

65. The Delhiites call *Hazrat Sultan ul Masha'ikh Khwajah* Nizamuddin Auliya, *Mehboob-e-Ilahi*, *Rahmatullah alaihi* (may the mercy of God be upon him!) Sultan Ji. His blessed tomb is situated near Humayun's tomb, 3 miles away from the Delhi Gate.

66. Quietly repeating an Attribute of Allah or a passage from the Holy Book.

67. In his later life, Bahadur Shah had become so tender-hearted that he would break into tears on every little thing.

68. A large masonry well, generally with winding steps down to the water, with landing places, chambers and niches in the surrounding walls [translator's note].

69. *Khadim* is the person who takes care of a tomb or shrine [translator's note].

70. The famous disciple of Hazrat Nizamuddin Auliya and the great Persian poet of India (d. AD 1325). Among the urban masses, he is still remembered for certain riddles and the *mandha*, a song sung at the departure of a bride on her wedding night [translator's note].

71. A *ser* (or *seer*) is of about two 1bs. in weight.

72. Please see note 32.

73. A Mughal emperor, popularly known as Muhammad Shah *Rangila*, or pleasure-loving (1719–1748) [translator's note].

74. Mirza Jahangir is the same prince due to whom the flower-sellers' festival began. After coming back to Delhi (from Allahabad), he again

started doing unbecoming things and was yet again sent to Allahabad where he passed away (AD 1821). Navvab Mumtaz Mahal, the Queen, had his dead body brought to Delhi and it was buried in a very beautiful marble *muhajjar* (enclosure) in *dargah* Nizamuddin.

75. Mirza Nili was the son of Shah Alam II (d. 1806). He was also buried in the marble enclosure of Mirza Jahangir [author's note]. His name was Izad Bakhsh, and he wrote Urdu poetry (*Sair ul Manazil*, 152, fn. vide *Majmu'ah-e-Naghz*, Vol. I, 303) [translator's note].

76. Jahan Ara Begum (1614–1681) was the daughter of emperor Shah Jahan. She had great faith in *Hazrat Shaikhul Masha'ikh* (Nizamuddin Auliya). Her tomb is in the marble enclosure at the foot of the tomb of Nizamuddin Auliya. The following couplet is inscribed on the tablet at the head of her grave:

Baghair-e-sabza naposhad kase mazar-e-mara
Keh qabr-posh-e-ghariban hamin gayah bas ast

Let no one cover my grave
With anything but green grass;
Only grass is sufficient
To cover a poor one's grave!

77. The tomb of Safdar Jang Mansur Ali Khan who was the governor of Oudh and the vizier at Delhi in 1748 (d. 1754) [translator's note].

78. Mirza Babur was the second son of Akbar Shah II. His English-style *kothi* still stands in the Qutab complex. One of its door opens in the *dargah*, one opens to the Jangli Mahal, and the third in the jungle towards the *jharna* (cascade).

79. Letters of the Urdu alphabet have been given numerical values which are mainly used to compose a chronogram. The practice is to form a brief sentence or phrase, the numeric values of all the letters in which add up to give the year, mostly according to the Hijri era, when the event took place. The Hijri era begins from AD 622, the year of the Prophet's migration from Mecca. Thus, the numerical value of the letters used in *Bab-e-Zafar payindah bad* add up to AH 1264, which corresponds to 1848 of the Christian era [translator's note].

80. It is a large and beautiful old building in the shape of a *jahaz* (sea-ship).

81. There is a small dome in the centre of this huge *talab* (tank). Beneath the dome there is a mark of a horse's hoof on a grey granite stone. There are many legends about this mark. Generally it is believed to be the mark of the hoof of the *buraq*, the mule on which the Prophet Muhammad is said to have ascended one night from Jerusalem to heaven, and thence returned to Mecca [author's note]. Another legend has it that it is the mark of the hoof of the horse of Ali, the son-in-law of the Prophet of Islam (*Sair ul Manazil*, 115) [translator's note]. It is so far away from the banks of the Talab that even the best of swimmers grow out of breath on their way towards it [author's note].

82. It is a small mosque on the banks of the Shamsi Talab. There are two *musallas* (places marked for saying prayers) in its courtyard. It is said that Khwajah Muinuddin of Ajmer (d. AD 1235; Mercy of God be upon him!) and Khwajah Qutbuddin Bakhtyar Kaki (d. AD 1236; Mercy of God be upon him!) said their prayers on these *musallas* [author's note]. It is also said that there is always a divine figure, though unidentified, in every congregational prayer said in this mosque [translator's note].

83. It is Mehrauli itself which is called the Qutab, a small village eleven miles away from Delhi. It had flourished well in the days of Mughal emperor, Muhammad Shah (Rangila). He was enamoured by the Qutab. Whenever it was cloudy, he left for the Qutab. He used to say, 'The clouds are our herald!'

84. Navvab Ghaziuddin Firuz Jang was the vizier of the kings of Delhi and the son of Asif Jah I (d. AD 1748). One must not confuse him with the Ghaziuddin Firuz Jang who got Alamgir II killed in Kotlah (in AD 1759) [author's note]. The killer was Ghaziuddin Imad ul Mulk (1737–1800) who was the grandson of Nizam-ul-Mulk Asif Jah I. Also see note 7 [translator's note].

85. This *barahdari* had no roof. It had fixed matted bamboo frames on which they had spread the flowery creepers. The whole roof was thus covered when flowers bloomed.

86. Sheikh Muhammad Ibrahim, poetically surnamed *Zauq*, a famous Urdu poet and guide of Bahadur Shah II in poetry (d. AD 1854) [translator's note].

87. The princes and the princesses both were taught several arts and skills in the Fort. Scarcely was there anyone among them who did not know archery or swordsmanship or handling of a gun, or how to ride or swim. Ever since the days of Babur (d. AD 1530), the Mughals, had been fond of water. If one takes the example of the Fort itself, half of it had been occupied by canals and cisterns.

88. Navvab Taj Mahal had a great say in the Fort. Though she was a *domni* (a woman belonging to the *dom* caste, who sang and danced before the ladies), ever since the king had admitted her in the palace, he had come entirely under her influence. Nothing could be done without her approval. At last, Navvab Zeenat Mahal overcame her and she was turned out in a way that she could never return to the Fort [author's note]. (For more on Taj Mahal and Zeenat Mahal see Dalrymple, *The Last Mughal*, 42–43; 336 and 448) [translator's note].

89. Red juice of a *kajira* flower and fine flour combined.

90. A black powder to tinge the teeth.

91. Literally *Tirmunhi* means 'one with an askewed face'. Her face had been inclined on one side due to a paralytic stroke [author's note]. According to another source her face looked askewed and swollen on one side because she kept too many betel-nuts on that side in her mouth (Aslam Pervez (ed.), *Qil'ah-e-Mu'alla ki Jhalkiyan* by Arsh Timuri (Delhi: Urdu Academy, 2001), 28; henceforth *Qil'ah-e-Mu'alla ki Jhalkiyan* [translator's note]. But she was a marvellous singer. Even Tan Ras Khan, the famous singer, tried to avoid her and had actually left after a wrangle with her [author's note]. Find out more on Tan Ras Khan in *Qil'ah-e-Mu'alla ki Jhalkiyan*, 54–58); also see Dalrymple, *The Last Mughal*, 43). It was she who used to sing the king's ghazals (a lyrical form of Urdu and Persian poetry) before him. Dildar was her younger sister. Both of them were *derah-darnis* (well-to-do courtesans with noble clients). Their granddaughters (daughters of daughters) were Doanni Jan and Kali Jan respectively and both of them lived in Delhi [author's note]. According to Shahid Ahmad Dehlavi [d. 1967], an essayist and founder-editor of *The Saqi*, Delhi and Karachi, the descendants of the said Doanni Jan and Chavanni Jan were Moti Jan and Naushabah Jan who held their classes in Delhi till 1947 when the former (Moti Jan) migrated to Pakistan and later passed away there. Naushabah Jan/Bai remained in Delhi. ('Dilli ke Arbab-e-Nishat', *The Fikr-e-Nau*, Zakir Husain College Magazine [Shahjahanabad Nambar, 1978], 257–60 [translator's note]).

92. *Khuda yare buvad, bi 'illah mubarak* (AH 1161 /1747–48; 31st year of accession of Muhammad Shah (AH 1131–1162); see *Sair ul Manazil*, 260, fn.; also 115 [translator's note].

93. This Gate was built by Sultan Ala'uddin Khilji (AD 1296–1316). It is just near the Qutab Minar and said to be matchless in beauty.

94. Literally guardian saint. Imam Zamin is the *'urf* (commonly known name) of Imam Ali Raza, the eighth Imam (AH 148–203/ AD 765–817) who lies buried in Khurasan. But some Muslims have made a tomb in his name in the Qutab just as they have made a Karbala in Delhi although the real Karbala is in Iraq [translator's note].

95. A big stone is placed on a rock towards the north about a mile away from Mehrauli. If even a child touches it, it shakes as if it will fall down [author's note]. (Bhim: lit. fearful; name of the second of the Pandava princes and said to be very powerful. A *chhitanki* is 1/16th part of a *ser* [translator's note].)

96. Karva Meetha Neem stands for sour and sweet neem tree. There is a neem tree on the tomb of some pious man near the Chhitanki. It is said that the daughter of Rai Pithora (i.e., Prithviraj, the Chauhan king of Ajmer and Delhi; d. AD 1192 (?); Majumdar, Ray Chaudhuri, and Datta, *An Advanced History of India*, 278 [translator's note]) had embraced Islam at the hand of that pious man. Her grave is under the neem tree. Leaves of the part of the tree on the pious man's tomb are sweet and those on the part of the woman's grave are sour.

97. This refers to the graves of the Pathan kings which are built on a raised platform.

98. These are graves of forty martyrs situated in front of the Auliya Masjid. It is said that they are never exactly counted for they are built in a disorderly way.

99. This is a building near Chahal Tan Chahal Man. One can hear people singing at night from this building.

100. Poetical surname of a Persian poet, Jalal Khan (d. AH 942/ AD 1535); *Sair ul Manazil*, 259, fn.; also 260 and 113–14. Also see Annemarie Schimmel, 'Islamic Literatures of India', in *A History of Indian Literature*, Vol. VII, ed. Jan Gonda (Wiesbaden: Otto Harrassowitz, 1973), 22 [translator's note].

101. This garden was the soul of the Qutab Complex. It was laid out so beautifully on the banks of the Shamsi Talab that, if seen from a distance, it looked as if hanging clouds had gathered there. Hardly could the rays

of the sun pass through them as it was so dense. Muhammad Shah, the king (1719–48) enjoyed many pleasures there as no other king could have even imagined. What more can I say than this: what is gone is gone; a life of relaxation and ease he led! The tomb of Mirza Shah Rukh, the son of Bahadur Shah, is built on a raised platform in the centre of the garden. The garden has grown less dense now.

102. The word is *tehband* which became *tehmad* and then *tehmat*. Shah Mubarak Abru the poet (d. AD 1733) says:

> *Abru ke qatl ko 'ajiz hu'e kas ke kamar*
> *Khun karne ko chale 'ashiq pe tohmat bandh kar*
>
> Tired of the lover she made herself ready to murder Abru;
> so after falsely accusing him, she is now on the move to kill him.
> [Author's note]

Actually, the poet has played here on a word occurring in the second semi-distich which may be pronounced differently with the change in the superscript (short vowel marks) on its first letter. If it is *tehmat* (that is, an affected *zer* beneath the first letter), it means 'a long loose cloth to be tied round the waist' as the first semi-distich here indicates, that is, it is firmly tied. But then *kas ke kamar* has also a pun. Literally, it is 'to tighten the cloth on the waist' but as an idiom it means 'getting ready'. If it is *tohmat* (that is, an affected *pesh* on the first letter), it means 'a libel' or 'an accusation'. If the reader of the couplet knows both the words (which the poet expects him to know), he may become doubtful as to which of them is more appropriate. And this is what the poet wants. Such play with words is known as *iham* or to be in doubt [translator's note].

103. The author has named the following dishes:

Puris: Thin cakes made of flour or wheat, fried in *ghee* or oil

Kachoris: Pastries made of flour and bruised pulse fried in *ghee* or oil

Bevris: Fried cakes of flour filled with or without pulse

Andarsa: A sweetmeat made of rice and flour kneaded into balls, then fried in *ghee* and covered with sugar

Suhal: Wheat flour kneaded with water and fried in *ghee* or oil, then made into flattened cakes

Kababs: Made of minced meat baked on grates

Parathas: Loaves generally round in shape, made with *ghee* and of several layers

Biryani: A dish of meat and rice

Muza'far: A kind of sweet dish; saffroned *pula'o*; and

Mutanjan-pula'o: Meat boiled with rice with spices and sugar.

104. Here, one who prepares and offers the *huqqah* (water-pipe for smoking tobacco) for a price [translator's note].

105. This army was raised by the king himself and consisted of the sons of the nobles of Delhi, tender-aged princes and the sons of the *salatin*. They were just boys but all of them were killed fighting near *ba'ota* (lit. a flag; a place near the ridge in Delhi) in the Mutiny (AD 1857). The old men of Delhi related their stories and cried over them. One does not know why there is no mention of the bachhera platoon in history—perhaps mention of a defeated army was not deemed fit.

106. Green was the royal colour of Delhi.

107. The eighth and most celebrated of the ten incarnations of Lord Vishnu is Lord Krishna [translator's note].

108. I have heard from my elders that the king was very fond of fireworks. Makers of fireworks had been employed on this occasion. No fair was held in the city when fireworks were not sent (as gifts) from the Fort. Competitions in the display of fireworks between the people of the Fort and the people of the city were also held. Two places were fixed for such competitions—the Shamsi Talab and the tank at the tomb of Hazrat Syed Hasan Rasool Numa [author's note]. He was a renowned Sufi saint d. AH 1103/AD 1691; *Sair ul Manazil*, 208, fn [translator's note].

Today there is no display of fireworks during the flower-sellers' festival. But at Rasool Numa they have kept the tradition alive and such competitions are still held there. What I had learnt from my elders has been confirmed now. In C. F. Andrews' biography of Munshi Zakaullah Khan of Delhi, he has collected information from the old inhabitants of Delhi about the conditions before the Mutiny. This book also mentions the fondness the King had for fireworks. It also throws light on the relationship between the king and the people of Delhi and their love for each other. He says that every old man, whether Hindu or Muslim, with whom he talked and sought information from, actually had tears rolling down from his eyes. It did not seem that they were narrating someone else's story. Rather it seemed as if they were talking of their own plight. This book has been recently published in 1929 by M/s W. Heifer & Sons Limited, Cambridge, and its price is seven rupees eight annas [author's note]. Maulvi Zakaullah of Delhi (1832–1910) was a student of the Old Delhi College. He became a Professor of Persian at Allahabad. The Government of India conferred on him the titles of *Shamsul 'Ulama* and Khan Bahadur for his scholarship. He translated and wrote more than 140 books on History, Geography, Mathematics, Ethics, Literature, Physics and Chemistry among others (Hamid Hasan Qadri, *Dastan-e-Tarikh-e-Urdu* [Agra: Lakshmi Narayan Aggarwal], 446–61) [translator's note].

109. This is the shrine of Hazrat Khwajah Qutbuddin Bakhtyar Kaki (d. AD 1235). He was the *khalifah* (successor) of Hazrat Khwajah Mu'inuddin Chishti of Ajmer (AD 1142–1236). Sultan Shamsuddin Iltetmish (1211–1236) [author's note]; ('hitherto called Iltutmish, it has now been established that his title was Iletmish'; M. Mujeeb, *The Indian Muslims* [Delhi: Munshiram Manoharlal Publishers, 1995], 34, fn. [translator's note]) had immense faith in him. Khwajah Qutbuddin met his death while he listened this couplet in a *qavvali:*

> *Kushtagan-e-khanjar-e-taslim ra*
> *har zaman az ghaib jan-e-digar ast*
>
> Those who are killed by the dagger of
> submission to God have always a life
> anew from The Unseen!

The rulers of Delhi built the walls and floor and marble lattices around his tomb. The walls were covered with *kashani* bricks (tiles). They also built mosques and the enclosures nearby. The grave itself is *kachcha*-built of unbaked bricks, but there are beautiful marble tombstones on the graves of others nearby. On one side there is a small mosque of marble and adjacent to it there are tombs of later kings of Delhi. In the centre there is the tomb of Shah Alam II (d. 1806) and on one side thereof is the tomb of Akbar Shah II (d. 1837). The other side was vacant. There the king Bahadur Shah II had made his *sardava* (grave which one prepares for oneself). He thought that after his death he could be laid to rest by the side of his ancestors. But who knew that his grave would be built at a place where, what to think of the proximity to the ancestors, there would be no one even to pray and invoke blessings for him! (He lies buried in Rangoon [translator's note].)

110. The people of Delhi have divided fireworks into two kinds: one is *jangi*, martial or relating to war, and the other *gulkari*, the flowery.

111. The big flying *anar* (a firework of the shape of a pomegranate) is called *hava'i*.

112. It is made by stuffing gunpowder in a long piece of bamboo wrapped up in entrails and closing them by the inner skin of an animal. It is really an art to play it. After lighting the gunpowder, they shake it and when it gets enough force they release it after winding it in the air. And thus this half a yard long piece of bamboo goes in the air with a loud noise and force. If the hand remains a bit low, and it finds its way amidst the spectators, then, God forbid, it may prove to do havoc, because one may break one's nose, or someone else may get his face bruised and still another's clothes may catch fire. If not handled properly, it becomes a curse instead of a firework.

113. First they make small, light-weight earthen balls. They are empty. On one side they make a hole and fill it with gunpowder. In the hole they put a small *chhachhundar* (itself a kind of firework) and throw the *lattoo* (top) upwards after kindling the *chhachhundar*. As the gunpowder catches fire, the top bursts with a loud noise as if a gun is fired. The *chhachhundar* is five or six inches long and is half an inch in diameter. It is restless like lightning and may change its direction when played.

114. *A khadanga* is called *khatanga* by the people of Delhi. This firework is too common and needs no introduction [author's note]. It is a paper cartridge filled with gunpowder with a *sitabah* (a tiny area of twisted thread to ignite the gunpowder) therein. The cartridge is fixed at the end of a thin reed-stalk, one-and-a-half-feet-long. While playing it, the reed-stalk is placed in a bottle with its bare end down in the bottle. Then the *sitabah* is lighted. It goes up in the air (higher than *chahka*) leaving a trail of colourful lights and then bursts with a little sound [translator's note].

115. The big *chhachhundar* is called *qalam*. Its gunpowder is so strong that when played, it cannot remain on the ground. Even after taking a bounce on water, it rises as high as 25 to 30 yards in the air.

116. A firework whose light when played, resembles sunlight [translator's note].

117. A firework in the shape of hanging, long, wreath-like string of flowers like those worn on the head by a bridegroom and it rains flowers when played [translator's note].

118. A firework resembling the jasmine, shooting flowers in the air like a fountain [translator's note].

119. A firework played while holding it in one's hand [translator's note].

120. *Charkhis* are crackers that go round and round on the ground when lighted [translator's note].

121. A pomegranate-like cracker as small as a small *batashah* (a sugar cake of a spongy texture, that is hollow within) [translator's note].

122. The tomb of Hazrat Khwajah Naseeruddin Chiragh Delhi (d. AD 1356) is in old Delhi at a distance of five miles from the Qutab and about seven miles from the Delhi city. He was the *Khalifah* (successor) of Hazrat Sultan ul Masha'ikh Khwajah Nizamuddin Auliya, and the title of *Chiragh Delhi* (Lamp of Delhi) was bestowed on him by his *pir* (guide). The locality where this tomb is situated is called Chiragh Delhi or Raushan Chiragh Delhi because of his tomb.

123. *Parathas* and *chhallas* were the only two things that were bought at the flower-sellers' festival and distributed as gifts from house to house in Delhi.

124. Although in a different context, C. F. Andrews had/rightly observed in 1929: 'The Mughal emperors, who came originally from Central Asia, as foreigners, into a strange country, not only acclimatised themselves, but also won the affection of the people over whom they ruled. But the alien element in British character seems almost incurably to remain, and the dislike caused by it appears to increase rather than decrease as time goes on ...' (*Zakaullah of Delhi*, 40) [translator's note].

Glossary

Abkhorahs	Earthen vessels to hold water
Aftabi	A firework whose light when played resembles sunlight
'Amamah	A sheet of cloth to be wound around one's head
Amarayyan	Mango-grove
Anar	A firework in the shape of a pomegranate
Andarsa	Fried sweet ball with sesame seeds in it
Angarkhas	Long tunics of long bodice
Angithee	Fire vessel
Annas	Nurses
Asil	Companions of noble stock
Bachhera Paltan	An army of tender-aged boys
Baheli	A small, two-wheeled vehicle without springs

Banat	A broad piece of cloth used for making uniforms for Turkish riders
Baniya	Owner of a grocery store
Ba'oli	A large masonry well, generally with winding steps down to the water, with landing places, chambers and niches in the surrounding walls
Barahdari	A hall with twelve doors
Belah	A reclaimed riverine land
Basant	Spring
Batashah anar	A firework in the shape of a pomegranate that looks like a small *batashah* (a sugar cake of a spongy texture, and hollow within)
Bhatiyara	Inn-keeper
Biryani	A dish of meat and rice
Bochah	A chair-*palki*, a kind of sedan
Bujra	Pleasure-boat
Chauhris	Fly-flaps
Chadar	A long piece of cloth
Chakkar	A sharp, circular missile firework
Chanwar	The tail of the Bos grunniens or the yak used as a fly-flap to fan away flies
Chaudol	A kind of sedan with two poles
Chehka	A firework
Chhachhundar	A firework five or six inches long and half an inch in diameter. It is restless like lightning and may change its direction when released from the base.
Chhaj-khajur	Fried sweetmeat in the shape of a date
Chhal	Fallen brick or part of a wall
Chhallah	A metalic ring to be worn on a finger
Chhapar khat	A bedstead with a tester and curtains
Chilam	A fire-pot
Chishti	An order of *sufis* (Muslim mystics)
Dab	Belt
Daglah	Quilted coat (platoon)

Dalan	Hall
Dargah	A shrine
Dari	Cotton carpet
Darogah	Superintendent
Daunas	Leaves folded in the shape of cups for holding sweetmeats
Deorhi	Porch
Dhol	Full drum
Diwali	A Hindu festival celebrated on the day of the new moon in the month *Kartik;* festival of lights
Diwar-giri	A lamp suspended against/attached to a wall
Doli	A litter; a type of sedan
Domni	A woman belonging to the *dom* caste, who sang and danced before the ladies
Doshakhah	Two-branched
Dupattah	A sheet of cloth to cover the head, shoulders and the bosom
Dur-bash	A large, beautifully coloured log, studded with small spears. It was kept ahead of the king's carriage to guard against any possible attack on him
'Eid	A festival that is celebrated after the month of Ramazan when the fasts kept during Ramazan are broken
'Eid ul Azha	A Muslim festival of sacrifice
Ghat	An area situated on the bank of a river, used for bathing or washing clothes
Ghoris	Wooden supports to hold the nae (pipe tube) of a *huqqah*
Ghungroo	An anklet with several layers of metallic bells strung together
Gondni	Sebetan plum tree
Gornet	Satin

Gulab-pash	A container used to sprinkle rose and fragrant keora water on guests; a symbol of welcome
Gulgula	Fried sweetmeat in the shape of a small ball
Gulkari	A firework that sparkles like flowers when played
Gurjans	Georgians
Habshan	Abyssinian
*Halva'*is	Confectioners
Havadar	A moveable throne on wheels; a seat placed on an elephant to ride on
Hava'i	A big flying *anar* in the shape of a pomegranate; it is made by stuffing gunpowder in a long piece of bamboo
Haveli	A mansion or house made of brick and stone
Holi	The spring festival of the Hindus
Huqqah	Smoking pipe
Isthan	Shrine
Jahi-juhi	A firework resembling the jasmine shooting flowers in the air like a fountain
Jangi	Martial or relating to war
Jarib	A staff with an iron point
Jharna	Cascade
Jha'u	A type of tree that grows in marshy or sandy land
Jogi	A person who strives to attain union with God; he renunciates all worldly pleasures (Fem: *Jogan*)
Kali	A small piece of cloth, triangular in shape (here)
Kalghi	Plume
Kaman	A bow
Karas	Massive gold rings to be worn on the wrists
Kashani brick	Tile
Karkhandar	An owner of petty cottage industry
Khadim	A person who takes care of a tomb or shrine

Khalifah	Successor of a sufi
Khansaman	Master of stores
Khas	Scented grass
Khatanga	A firework
Khavas	A favourite of royal ladies or princesses
Khwajah-sara	Eunuch incharge of a seraglio
Kotwal	The chief of the city police
Lagan	Trough
Lattoo	A top (a type of firework)
Luk ka chamra	Patent leather
Mahi	In mythology, it is the fish on which the earth is supposed to rest
Malhar	An old *raga* in Indian classical music that is associated with monsoon
Mandva	Bower
Manjholi	A medium-sized carriage
Masnad	Cushioned seat
Mehtabi	Open high terrace; a firework whose light when played resembles the moonlight
Missi	A powder, black in colour, used to tinge the teeth
Munder	A parapet or coping
Muqqaish	White silver thread
Musallas	Places marked for saying prayers
Muza'far	A sweet dish
Nae	Pipe tube
Nafl	Voluntary prayer
Nasri	A kind of firework
Naubat khanah	The chamber where the time of day or night was indicated by the beat of drums
Nechah	A tube
Nivara	A barge
Palki	A palanquin
Panj shakhah	Five-branched
Pankha	Fan

Panni	Thin metal leaf
Panvaran	A female betel-leaf seller
Papiha	A species of the cuckoo bird
Paratha	A loaf made with *ghee* and of several layers
Patka	Sash
Patris	Slabs
Pesh-qabz	Dagger
Phari-gatka	The use of shields and fencing sticks
Phisalna patthar	A stone that is slippery
Phulki	A small cake of peas meal fried in oil
Pishwaz	A long tunic of fine light cloth
Puri	A thin cake of meal fried in *ghee* or oil
Qalam	*A chhachhundar* bigger in size
Qalmaqani	A woman guard
Qil'ah-dar	Commandant of palace guards
Rakhi-bandhan	A festival celebrating the relationship between brothers and sisters
Rangila	Pleasure-loving
Rath	Oxen carriage
Raushan chauki	A small band of musicians
Salim shahi	Pump type shoes of pointed and a bit raised toe made of sheep/goat skin
Salono	A Hindu festival
Saqi	One who prepares and offers the *huqqah* for smoking tobacco for a price (here)
Sarangi	A stringed musical instrument
Sara pardah	A wall of canvas screens surrounding a cluster of tents
Sehra	A firework in the shape of long, hanging, wreath-like string of flowers like those worn on the head by a bridegroom; it rains flowers when played
Selah	A turban with one end hanging loosely from shoulders on the body
Ser	A weight equalling about two pounds

Shidanen	Plural of *Shidan* (feminine of *Shidi*, an Abyssinian)
Shikram	A camel-cart
Shuhda	Blackguard
Sitabah	A tiny piece of twisted thread to ignite the gun powder
Suhal	A thick, round, fried sweetmeat
Sukhpal	Palanquin
Suraj-mukhi	A type of fan, for shade
Surriyat	A girl who kept secrets
Takht-e-ravan	A moveable throne (erected on a platform carried on men's shoulders)
Tam jham	An open litter or chair carried by two men
Taqriz	An introduction of a book by way of commendation
Tarkash	Quiver
Tasbih khanah	An apartment or building for private worship
Tashah	A semi-spherical drum
Tehband/Tehmad/ Tehmat	A long, loose cloth to be tied round the waist
Tohmat	An accusation
Toshakchi	The superintendent of the royal store
Tukkals	Small paper kites
Turkan	A Turkish woman
Urdabegni	Armed female attendant in the harem
'Urf	Commonly known name
Ustad	Master
Vazifah	The practice of quietly repeating an attribute of Allah or a passage of The Holy Book
Ya Hazrat	Your Holiness (here)
Yaquti	An electuary

Bibliography

Andrews, C. F. 2003 [Reprint]. *Zakaullah of Delhi*. New Delhi: Oxford University Press.

Arshi, Imtiaz Ali Khan (ed.). 1944. *Nadirat-e-Shahi* by Abul Muzaffar Jalaluddin Muhammad Shah Alam II. Rampur: Hindustan Press.

Dalrymple, William. 2006. *The Last Mughal*. Delhi: Penguin/Viking.

Delhi College Magazine, *Dilli Nambar*, 1959.

Delhi College Magazine, *Firk-e-Nau, Shahjahanabad Nambar*, 1978.

Dehlavi, Shahid Ahmad. 1978.'Dilli ke Arbab-e-Nishat'. In *The Fikr-e-Nau*. Zakir Husain College Magazine (Shahjahanabad Nambar).

Firaq, Nasir Nazeer. 1986. *Lal Qil'e ki Ek Jhalak* or *A Glimpse of the Red Fort*. Delhi: Urdu Akademi.

Hali, Khwaja Altaf Husain. 1955. *Yadgar-e-Ghalib*. Allahahabad: Lala Ram Dayal Aggarwala, Shanti Press.

Hashmi, Noorul Hasan. 1971. *Dilli ka Dabistan-e-Sha'iri*. Lucknow: Idarah-e-Farogh-e-Urdu.

Husain, Ijaz (trans). 1978. *Tarikh-e-Shahjahan* by Banarsi Pershad Saxena. Delhi: Taraqqi-e-Urdu Board.

Majumdar, R. C., H. C. Ray Chaudhuri, and Kalikinkar Datta. 1950 [Second edition]. *An Advanced History of India*. London: Macmillan.

Monk, F. F. 1935. *A History of St. Stephen's College*. Calcutta: YMCA Publishing House.

Mujeeb, M. 1995. *The Indian Muslims*. Delhi: Munshiram Manoharlalal Publishers.

———. 1972. *Islamic Influence on Indian Society*. Delhi: Meenakshi Prakashan.

Naushahi, Gauhar (ed.). 1967. *Nata'ij ul Ma'ani by* Mehmood Beg Rahat. Lahore: Majlis-e-Taraqqi-e-Adab.

Pervez, Aslam. 2008. *Bahadur Shah Zafar*. Delhi: Anjuman Taraqqi Urdu.

Pervez, Aslam (ed.) 2001. *Qil'ah-e-Mu'alla ki Jhalkiyan* by Arsh Timuri. Delhi: Urdu Akademi.

Schimmel, Annemarie. 1973. *'Islamic Literatures of India'.* In *A History of Indian Literature*, Vol. VII, ed. Jan Gonda. Wiesbaden: Otto Harrassowitz.

Spear, Percival. 1940. Book for Schools, trans. Ishtiyaq Husain Qureshi, as *Asar-e-Dehli* in Urdu. Bombay/Calcutta/Madras: Oxford University Press.

———. 1969. *Twilight of the Mughals*. Delhi: Oriental Books Reprint Corporation, Delhi.

Qadri, Hamid Hasan. 1957. *Dastan-e-Tarikh-e-Urdu*. Agra: Lakshmi Narayan Aggarwal.

Qasmi, Sharif Husain (ed. and trans.). *1982. Sair ul Manazil* by Mirza Sangin Beg. Delhi: Ghalib Institute.

Qureshi, Kamil (ed.). 1986. *Bazm-e-Akhir* by Faizuddin. Delhi: Urdu Akademi.

DICTIONARIES

Dehlavi, Syed Ahmad. 1987. *Farhang-e-Asifiyyah*, Vol. II. Delhi: Taraqqi-e-Urdu Bureau.

Dehlavi, Maulvi Zafar ur Rahman. 1940. *Farhang-e-Istilahat-e-Peshah-varan*, Vol. II. Delhi: Anjuman Taraqqi-e-Urdu (Hind).

Platts, John T. 1977. *A Dictionary of Urdu, Classical Hindi and English*. Delhi: Oriental Books.

Urdu Lughat (tarikhi usul par), Vol. XII, Karachi: Taraqqi-e-Urdu Board.